THE COMMITTED SIDE CHICK 2

TINA MARIE

Cole Hart
SIGNATURE NOVELS

Mailing List

To stay up to date on new releases, plus get information on contests, sneak peeks, and more,

Go To The Website Below...

www.colehartsignature.com

ACKNOWLEDGMENTS

I would first like to thank God for giving me this gift of writing and for providing me with every blessing I have received thus far and will receive in the future.

I want to thank my family, my fiancé, Jay, for putting up with all the late nights and my crazy moods while I am writing. To my kids: Jashanti, Jaymarni and Jasheer, I want you to know that I work so hard so you can have it all.

To my Cole Hart Presents team, salute to all of you for keeping on the grind and staying positive. Cole, the fact that you wanted me on your team means more to me than you will ever know. Princess and Anna, I swear you ladies are just amazing and I love you! Twyla, there is no category for someone like you, any time I need a shoulder, a friend or a talking to you are there. I know you sick of me but I'mma love you foreverrrrr! Jammie and Reese, you two truly just make my life complete, and I thank God for giving me friends like you. I want to thank all of my Pen Sisters no matter what company you are in for all of the love, support and for always helping to push me to my next goal. I appreciate you all!

Ladora, you are the world's best little sister. I love you, and I believe in you always!

Natasha, we have been friends for what seems like forever, and now you're more like family. You could never be replaced in my life. You have seen me at my best and worst and still have my back. Oh, and you have learned to put up with all my moods. LOL. I love you, boo!

Natavia, only in a perfect world would I have thought that my favorite author would be my real-life friend. And even though this isn't a perfect world, I am so happy you became my friend. I value all the talks, laughs, wcc and advice. Love you soul sister (inside joke).

Coco, I didn't think I could write a dedication to you without crying- I was right. You are a bomb a** little sister. I would go to war for you with anyone. The way you love on my son and have never turned your back on me is everything. You're filled with positivity and joy, and I can't find the words to thank you. I love you!

Sunni there are so many days you have talked me off the ledge and just been a friend I love your whole life. I could never replace you. Your bestseller is right around the corner; I can feel it!

Nisey, Quanisha and Keke you three have been rocking with me since forever and are the best admins ever. I love how you love me but most of all, how you all have come to love each other. Tina, you may be new to the team, but you are a welcome addition! You ladies don't let me forget a thing and handle all the grunt work so that I can write. XoXo! To my test readers, Kristi, Sweets and Jammie, there would be no book without you ladies, you all are my blessings! Tootie and Liz I couldn't ask for better promoters~ one thing I learned in this business is it takes a team and finding the two of you completed my team.

To my Baby Momma Zatasha, even though we are both crazy Gemini's I still love you boo. Couldn't do this book ish without you!! And to all the Bookies, I appreciate the love and support you show all authors, not just me. It makes a difference having a place where we are respected, celebrated and offered endless support!

To my friends and family: I appreciate all of the love and support. My cousins, Claire, Dionne, Donna & Tanisha. My friends: Letitia, Natasha, Jennifer, Sharome, Shante, Diana and Kia. I'm truly grateful for you all, and I love you. To my best friend, there will never be enough letters in the alphabet to thank you for everything, so I won't even try.

To all of my fans, readers, test readers, admins and anyone who has ever read or purchased my work, shared a link or a book cover, you're all appreciated, and I promise to keep pushing on your behalf to write what you're looking for.

RUMOR

$\mathcal{I}$ let my eyes roam from the buzzing cell phone in my hand to the bed holding my baby girl. I thanked God she was ok, almost losing her shook me to my soul. Laya was hooked up to so many machines that the only thing visible was her tiny arm, her hand was swallowed up by Remee's larger one. He refused to leave her side no matter how many times I told him to go. His tall frame was stuffed into the small chair the hospital provided, and half his body was laid across the hospital bed. My phone went off again, and I kept my eye on Remee, silently praying he stayed asleep. "Hello," I answered as low as I could.

"The fuck I got to call your retarded ass more than one time? Shit, you called me first and then you want me to chase behind you. Rumor I don't want your ass, so I wish you would leave me alone." Just the sound of this nigga's voice made my skin crawl, but at the end of the day, he was A'Laya's father.

"Jordan, I was calling because our daughter almost died, but I guess you don't give a fuck about that either. And for the record, I definitely don't want your ass." My voice was getting louder because he was pissing me off. He was so ignorant, and I wished I wouldn't have called him to begin with, even though it was the right thing to do. "Now if you care your daughter pulled through and is at Stro-" I felt the phone being snatched out of my hand.

"Nigga, I don't know why the fuck you're calling Rumor, and I sure as fuck hope you don't plan on coming near A'Laya, or I can arrange a trip to the basement in this bitch." Remee's voice was cold as he spoke into the phone. Jordan must have hung up because he pulled the phone away from his ear and just looked at it in disgust. The expression on his face I had never seen before, and it made me want to run somewhere and hide. I swear the whole room froze with his icy stare.

"Yo bring your ass over here," he said as he damn near dragged me to the bathroom inside the room. My eyes got wide as he shoved me into the wall and glowered down at me. This nigga had his hands fisted like he was about to knock my head off and I wished I had some room to back up. "Rumor I let you get away with whatever the fuck you want. Like a nigga never check you on shit, but you not about to play with my daughter. The fuck you calling this nigga for?"

"Like it or not, Jordan is her father, not you. You have your own kid to worry about now," I snapped. Instantly, I regretted opening my mouth. I really just made it seem like I called Jordan on some petty get back shit, and that wasn't even the case.

He grabbed me up fast as hell and had his hand around my throat. "That nigga ain't a father to nothing over this way. He don't do shit for her, ain't been around her and you begging this fuck boy to come and see her. Rumor, you're smarter than that. You called this pussy two days ago, and he just called back. She could have been dead, and he wouldn't have cared. Hell, he doesn't care now. You can be mad about this shit with Jayda. Fuck, I'm mad about it. But don't you ever use that to play games with me and my shorty. Laya is mine, and I will body you, Jordan, or any fucking body else who tries to come between us."

He slowly put me back on my feet and unwrapped his hand from around my neck. He didn't really hurt me. I could feel him holding back every time his fingers started to get tighter. I wanted to keep defending my decision, but what was the point. Jordan didn't care about Laya. It looked like he never would. I let my body sag against the wall. This shit was all just too much for me. I felt like I was losing everything, including my sanity. Even though crying wouldn't help shit, I felt the tears fall. I was sobbing and holding my body. My life was one tragedy after another.

"You crying over this nigga? For real Ru,this bum ass dude who aint never been there got you breaking down! Remee roared as he punched the wall above my head. He looked at my phone he was still holding in his left hand and threw it at the mirror, causing it to shatter.

"Is everything ok in there," the voice of the nurse came out sounding shaky from the other side of the door. Remee refused to answer, and I couldn't do anything but cry. Instead of responding, he picked me up and slammed me against the door with a thud. I felt all the air in my body woosh from my slightly opened mouth.

"Rumor, if you think about getting back with him, I will kill you. If you bring him around my daughter, I will kill you," he hissed. His eyes bore into mine to the point where I had to look away. Now I heard more voices in the room, and I wondered if they called security. "Answer me," he snapped. I started to tremble, and he set me on my feet, his body moving closer. He dipped his head low like he was going to kiss me; instead, he jerked his head up and punched a hole in the door above my head. The hospital bill was going to be high as fuck the way he just tore these people's bathroom up. And I hope he knew he was replacing my fucking phone.

"A'Remee, open this damn door," a familiar voice called from the other side. I realized his mother was here, and most likely the rest of his family. Remee looked down at me like I betrayed him, and shit for a moment, I felt like I did. Then I remembered it was him that fucked me over.

"Why the hell would I get back with him?" I yelled. Remee had me fucked up. He was playing me like some weak bitch. I wasn't even crying over Jordan. I was sitting here crying over his ass. Wishing I could turn back the hands of time to before my baby was sick and before he moved on and had another kid behind my back, I closed my eyes.

"Because I left you," he stated simply like he was talking to someone slow. He stepped back some, and I finally felt like I could breathe, at least until his hands became fists again. "I know that's why you called him. You on some get back shit, trying to hurt me because I hurt you." My mouth fell open at the dumb shit he just said.

"Rumor, are you ok," his mother's voice called interrupting my moment of shock. Instead of answering her, my eyes closed into tiny slits as I glared at Remee. Just that fast, I went from feeling broken to just being pissed.

"Remee, I wouldn't get back with him to spite you. I would go find me a new nigga, and I'm going to find me a new nigga. And for the record, fuck you and Jordan." Before he could put his hands on me again, I opened the door and slipped out.

"Rumor, get the fuck back here," he boomed from behind me, but I ignored him. Everyone was standing there, staring at us when I burst into the room. The first thing I did was look towards my baby girl. Thank God the medicine had her knocked out, even with all the commotion. Remee damn near ran up on me as he left the room, but once he saw me move next to A'Laya, he let me be. I knew he was still mad the way his eyes were cold, and his face was a mask of fury. Since his mother was sitting in the chair next to Laya, I gently sat on the end of the bed. Amira came over and pulled me into a hug.

"Son, the fuck you and Ru got going on in this bitch. I had to slip the droopy titty ass nurse a stack to get the fuck out of here and not call security." Cahir was shaking his head and staring at Remee with an attitude.

"Don't worry about what the fuck me and her got going on. I keep telling you that shit. Get ya bread," he snapped, throwing money on the little hospital tray. I just knew the two of them were about to go at it and turn this bitch out, but Miss Layla shot them both a look before gently running her hand over Laya's curls.

"I ain't done talking to you," Remee barked damn near snatching me off the bed. I could see the stress creeping through the anger, and I almost felt bad for him. If Cahir wouldn't have pissed him off further he might have left me alone for the moment. "If you think you fucking wit' another nigga, I hope you know his ass gonna end up somewhere stinking."

I just nodded as tears escaped my eyes once again. I wasn't crying because he was physically hurting me, even though his hands had a grip on my arms. All the emotional shit was catching up to my ass in a big way. As soon as Rem saw my tears, he damn near dropped me. Once my feet touched the floor, he pulled me into his arms and let me cry into his chest. "Come on Rumor, don't do that shit ma, I know I fucked up." He knew me so well. It was like he could read me; he always knew when I was in pain. Or maybe it was because he always caused my pain. I tried to push him away, but he just held me tighter. "Remee, just go see your son. You shouldn't be here with us right now."

"Rumor, fuck all of that, I don't even know if that lil nigga mine. My daughter almost died, I ain't leaving her for any fucking body, not even ya ass or my mama. That's on God!" Before I could respond, the hospital room door opened. I

5

thought it was a nurse, but when my head turned, I saw a female rush inside instead. I heard Remee curse under his breath as she damn near ran up on him and me.

I knew right away it was Jayda. I recognized her from her profile picture. I had memorized every detail of her face after she messaged me. Even after just having a baby, she was flawless. Her Victoria Secret pajama set hugged her curves, and her long jet-black weave was flowing effortlessly down her back. Her face was a smooth mocha and looked untouched, not a blemish or scratch on it. I could understand how Remee was weak for her, how he could walk away from me for her. Her beauty was stunning and only interrupted by the long colorful ghetto nails and crazy eyes.

"Oh, for real Remee, you don't know if the little nigga is yours? Guess what he is actually yours, and you belong with us not some kid who isn't even ya baby!" She was screaming so loud I knew security would be joining us soon. I watched as Remee's eyes filled with rage, and I wondered would he be catching a murder charge. Sire and Cahir grabbed him, already knowing how his temper was set up. I could say one thing, Remee had fucked me over plenty of ways, but when it came to A'Laya, no one got a pass.

"Bitch what the fuck are you smirking for? I will beat ya sorry ass. You must have the wackest pussy in the world the way this nigga stayed cheating on you. Or was he ever cheating on you? Maybe he was cheating on the other women in his life. You're just a convenient piece of pussy. One that's always around, a professional side piece, that's it. You couldn't even give him a child!" Jayda was clapping her hands and after each word she was damn near yelling, but I didn't hear shit else she said after she mentioned me not being able to give Rem a child. Thinking about losing my son and Laya being Jordan's and not Remee's set off something inside of me. I had had enough.

I walked towards Jayda as she kept talking shit. Grabbing her by her extra-long bundles, I started punching her in the face. Every time I heard her cry out, it gave me satisfaction. Seeing the blood gush from a cut under her eye and from her now crooked nose caused me to feel a rush and keep going. For the moment, I didn't care about shit. I didn't even care about the fact that my child was sleeping in the room, that she just had a baby, or that this was a hospital. She had become every woman that Remee ever cheated on me with, ever hurt my feelings with, and she was going to pay. I saw Sire move forward to stop me, but Rumor grabbed him and damn near flung him to the ground.

"Naw, let her get that shit out." He said as he watched in approval as I beat her ass. Suddenly I stopped, everyone in the room was looking at me. I was ashamed that I was doing this shit in front of all these people, and worse my daughter. Miss Layla had somehow moved even closer to A'Laya and had a look of sadness on her face. Amira was next to her; fists bawled up ready to jump in and save me like always. Except this time, I didn't need her. Cahir had a blank look on his face, but I could see the always present anger deep in his eyes. I felt like I had lost myself behind a man. I was just talking shit about another nigga earlier, but maybe it really was time to move on.

"Really Remee, you just going to let her fuck me up and I just had your son? You a real ain't shit ass nigga." Jayda stood there hugging her torso, blood mixing in with her tears and snot.

"How the fuck she even knew where to come and find you," Cahir asked. His cold eyes were boring into Jayda's. If she knew what was good for her, she would tell the truth. Instead of speaking, her eyes shifted to the left towards Shay's snake ass. I wanted to beat her ass too, but at the moment the fight had left me.

"It's time for you to go," Cahir said calmly. A little too calm. Not wasting any time Jayda dragged her worn-out body towards the door. Every few minutes she would look back at Remee, I guess hoping he would come to her rescue. She really didn't know him well, Rem wasn't built like that. He may have broken my heart too many times to count, but these bitches would never get the best of him. He treated women like shit, maybe due to his guilt for always doing me dirty or because he was just one of those niggas.

Finally, her hand opened the door, and she stood still, her eyes roaming the room until they landed on me. An evil laugh escaped her swollen lips, causing me to look her way. "Bitch, I hope you're ready for the get back. I promise you will pay for this!" The door closed softly as she made her exit. Remee reached out to pull me in his arms, but I snatched my body away. He let out a deep sigh and ran his hand over his face, after a few minutes he left the room to follow behind his baby mama.

REMEE

"*Aww*, baby daddy I knew you cared," Jayda spat as I walked up on her. She still had a look of pain on her face, but it was now mixed with a smile. I swear this hoe was dumber she looked. She thought she won some grand prize by supposedly giving me a baby. That baby wasn't going to change shit with her and me. The way I felt she would be lucky if I acknowledged the kid even if he was mine. She played a game that she wasn't ever going to win. She could never take the spot Rumor had in my life. No bitch could.

Grabbing her arm, I shoved her against the wall hard. I was losing control and fast. When I spoke, it came out as a growl, and I felt Jayda cringe. "Bitch, I let the little bullshit threat you made the other day slide because I thought it was the pregnancy fucking up your judgement. But I can see you just want a nigga to put hands on you. Let's get some shit clear right now. Rumor and my daughter are off-limits. Don't say shit to them, about them or even near them. If you even think about my shorty, I will kill you. I don't give a fuck about you in the least and if we have a baby together that shit doesn't change anything, because to be honest wit you, I never wanted the lil nigga anyway."

She stood there with tears in her eyes, and her feelings all hurt. But I wasn't moved, her slick ass mouth got her that. Shorty was pretty as fuck on the outside, but in my eyes, no one was prettier than Rumor. Jayda was just something to do because I could. Her cute face and wet pussy fucked shit up, and all I felt was rage and regret when I looked at her. "Show me the baby and shut the fuck up." She slowly made her way to the elevators, and I followed her back to the maternity ward. The whole way there, I considered snapping her neck and dumping her body somewhere in this hospital. She opened the door to her room and crawled in the bed. Her dumb ass was there playing with the sheets and blankets, and I didn't see a baby in sight. "Jayda, did you even have a baby? Because I don't see his ass anywhere."

She rolled her eyes and slowly pushed a button on the side of the bed. "Yes Miss Drew, can I help you?" A voice called from the intercom.

"Nurse please bring my son into the room. His father is here to see him." Her statement was finished with a smirk, and all I could think about was murking this bitch. The urge to get rid of her got stronger every time she spoke.

"Yes, ma'am," she responded, and I knew this was it. I felt my heart pounding in my ears as I waited for the nurse to bring him in. Maybe this was all a joke, and it wasn't my kid. I prayed I could tell just looking at him that he wasn't mine. I should have thought about having a test done before I pushed Rumor away. The knot in the pit of my stomach was so strong I just knew I fucked up and that this baby was going to turn out to be mine. The minute the door opened, and the staff wheeled him in, I knew he was my shorty. He favored his mother but had my honey-colored eyes, my nose and even a dimple in his left cheek. I was struggling to think, to breathe. I felt like someone shot me in my chest. This was some shit you couldn't take back or hide from the world.

"Nurse, can you bring the birth certificate paperwork so he can sign," Jayda said causing me to pull myself together. My head shot up, and I gave her a warning look. She had a huge smile on her face like she won the damn lotto. In a sense she just fucking did. But I still needed proof, the way she fucked the town my brother or cousin could be the daddy.

"Nurse, don't bring shit until I get a DNA test. Matter of fact, let's make that happen right now." The nurse didn't look surprised, hell if anything she looked sorry for me. I wondered what kind of hell Jayda had put the staff through the past twenty-four hours. She looked like an ignorant hoe.

"I will be back with the swab in one moment." I nodded, distracted by the small cries coming from the little plastic bassinet. I moved closer and felt numb looking at him. If I hadn't fucked up years ago, I would have had a son with Rumor. But I never got to see my son take his first breath, hear his cries or see him open his eyes. This shit hurt in a different way. This baby was like my kryptonite. He stopped crying as soon as he saw my face and just looked at me. His small eyes reflecting mine, almost showing an understanding of who I was, even though I knew he ain't have the capacity for that yet. The little tag with the baby's name caught my eye. I couldn't see shit but red after I saw Remee McKenzie Jr. in black sharpie on the white card. I snatched that shit off and ripped it to pieces.

"Remee what the fuck is your problem," Jayda screeched damn near jumping off the bed. For someone who just pushed a baby out her coochie, she sure bounced back fast as hell. She just jumped up like a fucking super-hero coming to save the day.

"Bitch that ain't his fucking name. Hell, that ain't even my right name. I already have a Jr. So, pick a new name." I talked slow hoping she would get the point and fast.

Her face twisted up as she stalked her way towards me. "Remee, you don't have any fucking kids. That little girl ain't yours and I sure as hell know you don't have a son. And I hope you not talking about the baby Rumor let ya bitch kick up out of her. His little ass is dead and gone…"

Before she could continue, I had my hand around her neck and started choking her out. I could still see the name A'Remee Najai McKenzie Jr., on my sons grave. He may have been dead, but the memory of him would never go away. "That's my fucking son you are talking about." I roared, shaking her like a rag doll. "I will kill you right now and go to jail for it. When it comes to my kids, I don't give a fuck. That's my namesake, my son, don't ever fucking speak on him again." Her eyes were big as she clawed at my hand, trying to get me to ease up. All she could get out was little mewling noises, she sounded like a hurt cat. Suddenly her baby started wailing, causing me to snap out of it. I dropped her on the floor like the trash that she was.

"I'm sorry, I was wrong. That was taking it too far." She sobbed as she crawled to the side of the bed and pulled herself up. Now she felt like she was taking shit too far, her dumb ass took it too far when she snuck and had a baby behind my back. She had a hard time getting on the bed, but I wasn't helping her ass one bit. Only thing I did was roll the baby closer so she could handle him once she got settled. Wasn't his fault his mother was retarded as fuck. She laid there for a few minutes struggling to catch her breath and finally picked him up.

"Fuck you being sorry, it was almost lights out for you, and next time your kid won't save you. Learn to watch ya fucking mouth."

"I hate your ass," she hissed, causing me to give her the side-eye. What the fuck was she mad for, shit she trapped me. I didn't want to be stuck with her ass for the next eighteen years. She caused all of this now she hated me. I wanted to smack the fucking taste out of her mouth. If she stayed alive for the next decade, it would be a miracle.

"Bitch I hate your stupid ass too." Before I could say anything else the door opened again, but instead of the nurse an older version of Jayda strolled in, her nose turned up when she saw me. A second later I noticed her ratchet ass cousin Lolo slip in behind her.

"Oooh hey baby daddy, I didn't know you were here," Lolo squealed, her long bright pink fingernails waving around. I couldn't tell if she was happy for her cousin or herself. She was posing herself and shit like I was interested. One thot ass family member was enough, so no thanks. She was a pass around anyway and half the crew done buss down her throat.

"Hey, mom. Thanks for bringing my bag," Jayda said as the lady set a duffel bag down on the end of the bed and rolled her eyes. Suddenly her gaze shifted back to me, and I knew she was about to be on some bullshit.

"So, this is the daddy, huh? You don't look broke, not one bit." She had come to stand in front of me and was analyzing the Rolex I had on, along with my chain and diamond earrings. Her intense inspection ended at my Gucci sneakers. "So, if you can afford to dress like this, why is it that my daughter and her kids are still living in the ghetto?" She stared at me, waiting for a response. I guess I was supposed to feel some kind of way about her scamming, hoe ass daughter's situation. The fuck outta here.

"Auntie don't worry he won't be like her other baby daddies. This is one of the McKenzie brothers. So I know he is going to cash out on Jayda and the kids," Lolo said damn near jumping up and down in excitement. She ended her outburst with a hi-five with Jayda and a hand motions of someone throwing money.

"Kids? Shorty you got more kids? Damn you trap they daddies too?" I let out a bitter laugh. "For the record, I don't look broke, because I ain't broke, and I sure as fuck ain't cashing out on any bitches. But if he is mine, I will take care of him."

"Of course, she has kids. How do you have a baby with her and not know her son and daughter?" Her mom looked appalled. But she couldn't have been more than me. What kind of mother be in the club seven nights a week and got kids at home? She was damn near a resident in my clubs, that's how I met the trick.

"Well, that's simple because your daughter is a hoe. She sucked my dick in my club a few times than I let her move up to fucking me now and then. She played some games to get pregnant, and I just found out she potentially had my kid two weeks ago. She doesn't even know my name. So, you're asking the wrong person all of this shit. Talk to her loose pussy having ass." Her mother gasped and turned to address her child. "And don't be acting all fucking shocked, she had to learn that loose pussy behavior from somewhere." I was done with the conversation, so I hope she knew not to say shit else to me.

I stood off to the side of the room, watching her mother and her having some hushed ass conversation. Her cousin stared at my dick print the whole time, making me feel uncomfortable as fuck. Finally, the nurse came and swabbed my cheek. As soon as she was done, I turned to get the hell out of there. "Your leaving?" Jayda asked like an idiot. How sway she thought I was staying to chill with her.

"Fuck yea, if the results come in that he is mine we can set up some child support payments from there." My voice held a note of finality, and nothing else was said. I damn near ran up out of there. I felt like I was suffocating. Just a few weeks ago I was about to marry the girl I loved and keep my dick under control and just that fast all my plans were ruined. I lost Rumor. I could see it in her eyes when she pushed me away today. That was the real reason I let her go, she had already dealt with enough crazy bitches on my behalf. And I knew Jayda wasn't going to leave shit alone. I was going to have to stay fucking her up. Rumor wasn't going to keep putting up with all this drama forever, and this bitch was in my life for fucking ever.

Slowly I walked back to the children's ward, my heart heavy. I noticed everyone but Amira seated in the waiting room. "Laya ok?" I asked fear creeping in my heart.

"She good," Cahir said, barely looking my way. I knew he was pissed, but like I said before, this shit wasn't his business. Hesitating, I stood outside the door listening to my sister trying to cheer Rumor up. Her tiny laughs were forced, not the ones I was used to. I wanted to walk away and leave, not deal with what came next. But I was a man, and I had to tell her this baby was most likely mine. Just that fast, her forced laughter turned to tears causing me to run my hand over my face and close my eyes. Hearing a snicker caused my eyes to open quick.

"Bitch, what the fuck is funny," I barked as I stormed over to the corner Shay was standing in. She just smirked and shrugged her shoulder. I hated that Sire had a kid with this hoe. "Sire, get your girl before I put my fucking hands on her." I was mad as fuck, but this nigga was still in his phone texting away like no one was talking to him. "Nigga, it's like you don't hear me talking to you," I snapped.

His head snapped up, and he looked confused. I knew it was that other shorty he had been fucking wit who had his attention. Hopefully, she would hurry and replace this smut Shay. "I'm going to check her ass." He said glaring Shay's way.

I made sure to bump that bitch before stepping back. "Yo, I'm out."

* * *

I LEFT THE HOSPITAL BUT DIDN'T GO HOME. I DROVE AROUND THE city for hours trying to clear my head, but that shit wasn't working. I smoked a few blunts back to back and parked down the street from the hospital. I ignored the calls coming through on my lines. I just needed everyone to leave me the fuck alone. I watched the sun go down, and the crackheads flood the streets. They came out after dark in large numbers and scattered in the morning like roaches. I looked at them for hours, rushing back and forth, begging and selling everything but the clothes off their back. Their only worry in the world was getting that next hit. Nothing else even mattered. If I was a weak ass nigga, I would try that shit just to forget about all my problems.

I stayed that way for hours; my thoughts still dark as fuck. Finally, I gave up and drove into the hospital garage. I needed to be near Rumor and my daughter, even if I was going to be hurting her for what I prayed was the last time.

I was happy my family had finally left. I was sure my mom would be back in a few hours though. She acted like Rumor was her kid and was probably ready to whoop my ass. Since the failed proposal, I had been avoiding my mom as much as possible. I just wasn't in the head space to have her get in my ass about my fucked-up life.

I opened the door to my daughters' room slowly hoping her and Rumor were asleep. But no such luck, Ru lifted her tear-stained face off the pillow where she laid next to my baby girl. Even though my shorty was beyond stressed, she was still pretty as fuck. I wanted just to snatch her and Laya up and run away, leave all this shit behind. "She was asking for you," Rumor whispered before looking beyond me at the wall.

I walked to the bed and lifted her chin, so she was looking at me. I wanted to know what she was thinking, feeling. "He's yours, isn't he?" She asked, her voice trembling. I couldn't even find the words, so I nodded. I refused to lie to her, and even though I hadn't gotten the test back. I knew in my heart I had fathered that baby. "Why Remee, why did this happen to us?"

She tried to turn away from me, but I snatched her out the bed and held her in my arms. She didn't fight me, just laid her head on my chest as I sat down with her. I didn't know what to say, that I was selfish, because really it was the truth. I wanted to have her as my unofficial girl while I fucked whoever just because I could. "You know a nigga sorry right? I didn't do this shit intentionally; it was supposed to be you and me." I said. I sat there the rest of the night holding her as her tears wet up my chest, causing my heart to ache.

SIRE

I admit I wasn't paying attention to much since I had got here. The first thing I gave my attention to was making sure my niece was ok. After that, it was all a blur until I heard Remee say he would leave Tayari motherless. I had spent the past few hours calling Bella, texting Bella and just straight up pleading my case. But she wasn't saying a word. I had no idea why she wasn't at home earlier, in the bed naked where I left her. Or why she was working at a location that wasn't hers. Had I known we would have never stopped. We should have pushed on to Taco Bell or some shit. I fucked up, and I could see it in her eyes when she spotted Shay and me. But I guess this shit was going to come out sooner than later, especially since her people had seen us in the club together the other night. I was just waiting on her to run her mouth to Bella, but I guess she hadn't gotten to it yet.

I really didn't give a fuck about Shay being there with me. I had every intention of speaking to Bella. Of somehow trying to make it right, but then I got the call about A'Laya, and we had to run up out of there. "Lil nigga, it's like you don't fucking hear me talking to you," Remee snapped causing me to look up from

18

the last text I had sent to Bella. "Control your bitch before I do." Shay was standing off to the side smirking and giggling without a care in the world. Remee made a point to walk close to where she was standing and bumping the shit out of her.

"Oww," she cried out dramatic as fuck as her head bounced off the vending machine she was standing near. I didn't bother hiding the smirk that I had on my face. Her retarded ass deserved that shit. "Really, Sire? You're not going to do anything?" She screeched.

"Man, let's go," I demanded as I ran my hand over my face. This bitch stayed fucking up my life. Bella wasn't fucking wit me, and now Remee was pissed. And I knew how he got when shit wit him and Rumor wasn't going good. His mood was more than fucking foul.

"But I want to go and see Jayda, and the baby," she pouted. "Come on, he is your real nephew so let's go visit." I was in the middle of sending Bella one last message telling her if she didn't call back, I was about to kick her door in when she uttered that dumb shit. I looked at Shay like she was slow.

"Bitch, I said we are leaving. This ain't no fucking visit animals in the zoo day. Fuck that girl, see her on ya own time. Right now, you on mine and I got shit to do. And that little boy ain't nothing to me until my brother tells us something different." She stomped out of the waiting room, leaving me to pick up my sleeping daughter, who was in my mothers' arms.

"Son, I just don't know with that one. Where the fuck you find her ass at? I guess the same place Remee found her thot ass friend," she sighed as I kissed her on the cheek.

"I know ma, I ask myself that shit every day, but I'm stuck with the bitch now. I will see you later. Keep me posted on Laya." I hurried after Shay. I needed to drop this bitch off so I could hurry and get to my girl. Whether she knew it or not, Bella was still my girl.

"Sire, you need to get on board with Jayda being a part of

this family. She has a baby with your brother, and this misplaced loyalty you and your family have for Rumor and her kid has to end. They are nothing to ya'll that ain't Remee's kid, and Rumor isn't his wife. Now hurry up and drop me off at home so I can come back and see my friend." Before she could open the door to my truck, my sister snuck the shit out of her.

"Bitch, you always running your mouth. You must have wanted to suck Remee's dick the way you stay worrying about his girl and daughter. He don't want you or ya raggedy-ass friend. We will never accept her, the same way we don't fuck wit you." She gave her two more face shots for effect then opened the door for her. Shay stood there looking dazed, her right eye swelling. "Bitch I opened the door for you to get in," Amira barked causing Shay to go sit inside. Lil sis was a trip.

"Damn Tyson, you out here creeping around in the parking garage looking for fights," I said laughing as I strapped my daughter into her seat and shut the door. Her mama was in the front seat checking her face in the mirror, looking like the drama queen that she was. She should have kept her fucking mouth closed if she wasn't ready to fight.

"It's not even like that big brother. I came to give you Tayari's blanket. She left it inside. The rest was just good timing." She went to give it to my baby as my phone rang. Seeing Bella's name, I clicked answer fast as fuck.

"Bells you good?" It was a stupid ass question, but I didn't know what else to say to her. I was just happy as hell she hit me back.

"Nigga don't be asking me if I'm good. No, the fuck I ain't good. You fucked me over. I knew you was a dog ass nigga and that's why I asked you to leave me alone when you saw me. I heard the stories about you and all these different women over the years, and now I'm glad I walked away from you even if I needed you. Because I would have been just as hurt as I am now. Don't be telling me you are busting in my fucking door and stop calling and texting me. You didn't just hide a fuck buddy or some random hoe. You got a whole woman and child. I can't get past that." I could hear the heartbreak in her voice, and it made me feel defeat and panic at the same damn time. I couldn't lose Bella; she was the one, and I wished I would have just been honest with her from jump. *Fuck!*

"Come on ma, don't say no shit like that. I swear it ain't as bad as it looks. I never wanted to hurt you. I don't want to be with no one else. Just let me come and explain shit to you. Give me a chance." I didn't even care that I sounded like I was begging, or that my sister was standing there all in my mouth.

"I don't know Sire. I trusted you, and now I don't even know what to do." I felt like I was breaking her down a little since she sounded so unsure.

"Sire can we go now, you rushed me, and now you're on the phone like you have nothing better to do." Shay was loud as fuck through the window she had opened, and I could tell by the way Bella gasped on the other end she heard her. I muted the phone before addressing Shay.

"Yo, close the damn window, Shay. What the fuck you doing in my business? I will be ready when the fuck I'm ready." She huffed and hit the button on the window.

"Wow Sire, you really snuck and answered my call while your girl was waiting on you. Don't fucking hit my line again. We done."

I hit unmute fast as hell as I groaned. "Bella we not over, and don't hang up this fucking phone," I barked, but it was too late, all I heard was the click of her ending the call. "Fuck," I yelled out loud as I punched the side of my truck.

"What was that all about," Amira said, her eyebrow raised. "I need to meet the girl on the other end of that call who got my brother out here about to go crazy. I just hope it ain't another one of those," she seethed looking towards Shay.

"You gonna meet her. Bella is the shit. Smart, pretty, a good mom, and she can cook. She got my fucking heart for real."

"Oh yea, send her to the shop for a free hairdo. I can't wait to find out more about this one." She was grinning from ear to ear and hopping around like I had found a match for her instead of myself.

"Do me a favor, take Tayari home wit you for the night. I will give you ten racks." My little sisters' eyes lit the fuck up like it was Christmas. As much money as she had, and she was still excited at the prospect of more. I swear we created a monster with this girl and her spending habits.

"Transfer that shit now and we on our way to the crib." I took out my phone and made the transfer from my checking to hers. She heard a ding and checked her Apple watch. "Nice doing business with you. For the record, I would have taken my niece anyway." She snatched opened the back door and pulled my baby out fast as hell. Holding my baby girl close, I watched her until she made it back into the door of the hospital.

"Don't spend all that money in a day, Mira," I called out to her before I hopped in my truck and peeled off. I was hoping for a silent ride to the crib, but I should have fucking knew better.

"Why the hell would you have your sister take our daughter if we are going home?" I wanted to ignore her, but she was like a fly, always buzzing around, and I had to either respond or squish her ass.

"I said you was going home, not me. Now is there anything else you want to fucking bother me about?" I was in a foul ass mood, and if she kept pushing me, I was leaving her ass on the side of the fucking road.

"No, that ain't fucking all. Sire, what is happening to us? I love you, and I don't know what else to do to keep you happy, but I can tell you are not. I swear I am willing to change, just tell me what to do." She started sniveling, causing me to sigh in frustration. I checked my phone for the tenth time since I started driving, hoping to see a message from Bella. Even if she was cussing me out, that was ok. I became more agitated when I saw no new messages.

"Sire, are you cheating on me?" Shay asked, holding her breath for my response.

"Yea, I'm cheating on you, I've always cheated on you, so stop acting like you don't know whats up," I answered before turning the music up. I wasn't into lying, and Shay knew I been cheating our whole relationship, so I wasn't sure where the questions were coming from now. I noticed her sitting there with a stunned look on her face. It was almost like I had slapped the shit out of her. Shorty turned my music down, and I was happy we had almost made it to the crib.

"Do you love her," she asked, her voice sounded sad as fuck and for a minute I felt guilty for being in love with someone else. All these years Shay had never complained about me getting my dick wet from time to time. Or even when she had to fight randoms about her man, hell she seemed like she enjoyed that shit. But the fact she was asking this shit now, meant she knew how I felt about Bella and that she was more than just sex. Pulling into the driveway, I parked and looked over at Shay. She was ratchet as fuck, but she still gave me my first kid. I tried to respect her, I mean yea I got topped off and broke a few bitches off with some dick. But the shit I had going on with Bella was different. Way more than a one-night stand or a chick I just hit up to fuck. Bella could get my money, my heart any fucking thing she wanted.

"Shay, just go inside ma, I got shit to do." It was on the tip of my tongue to tell her hell yea I loved her. But I didn't have it in my me to deal with her broken heart right now.

"Go get my daughter; I want her home. You need to come home with her if you want to see her. You got me fucked up Sire. You and that bitch will never be happy. I swear you won't."

"Yo get the fuck out of my whip with that dumb shit. I ain't going to get any fucking body. You barely know how to take care of our daughter and never have her with you. So, keep those empty threats over there before your mom be out here buying a black dress. Stop fucking playing with me!" I grabbed her chin hard and looked in her eyes when I said the last part. She needed to know I was serious as a heart attack when it came to my kid. Reaching around I pushed open the door and damn near shoved her out.

I watched her talk shit the whole way to the door before slamming it hard, like I gave a fuck. I sped off to Bella's crib. Shorty was going to hear me out tonight no matter what. I screeched into a parking spot scaring the shit out of one her neighbors who was hanging around outside. I hated that she lived here. It wasn't in the hood, but there was a lot of hood shit going on. After giving his buster ass a look, he went back to minding his own business. I could see all the lights off except the one in Bella's bedroom, so I knew she was still up. I didn't bother knocking, just used the key I had made one day when I borrowed hers and let myself in. I was happy as fuck I didn't have to kick in the door, scaring Jael wasn't on my list of things to do.

I didn't even bother taking my shoes off, I just crept up the stairs and headed straight to her bedroom. She wasn't awake and for that I was grateful. Instead, she was curled up hugging on her pillow like it was her new nigga. I wanted to shoot that mother fucker out from under her. I wanted Bella to be hugged up under me, not the fucking pillow. I kicked off my shoes and took my jeans, hoodie and t-shirt off. Before I slid in the bed with my girl, I decided to go and check on Jael. She was in bed fighting with the covers, and shit she looked like she had won. I fixed the pink and white sheets and blankets and placed a kiss on her head.

Hitting the light in Bella's room, I eased in the bed beside her, causing her to cry out in her sleep. I pulled her in my arms and pushed the pillow off the bed. She didn't even resist, her body melted into mine, and I placed light kisses on her neck and whispered, "I love you," in her ear. She settled down and was into a deep sleep within a few minutes, and I followed right behind her. We could talk in the morning.

I felt something hit me in the head, and I shot up. "Yea nigga, that's right, wake the fuck up. I don't know how you got in, but I'm sure I was clear when I said I ain't fucking wit you," Bella snapped in a low voice. I knew she wasn't trying to wake up baby girl. I smiled at how sexy she was when she was angry, at least until she threw my other Timberland boot at my face, busting my whole lip open. I tasted blood, and for a minute, I almost forgot who she was and beat her ass.

I got up and made my way towards her, except she kept backing up. Finally, when she had nowhere else to go, she raised her tiny hands into fists. It was cute to watch her squaring up with a nigga. Her breasts were heaving up and down as she breathed hard from anger. Her tiny silk sleep shirt rode up a little as she raised her arms into a fighting position, and I could see her bare skin. I tried to grab for her, but she started swinging on me like we was in the streets. "Arabella, stop fighting me ma. You can be mad, but I'm ya future, and you need to hear ya man out."

"Sire, leave me alone. You lied, and you played the shit out of me. Just like the last nigga I was with." She suddenly stopped hitting me and turned towards the door to try and make a run for it. I grabbed her and threw her over my shoulders all while she was bucking her body and scratching up my back.

"It's all good bae, let that shit out," I coached laughing a little. I never thought quiet ass Bella would be fucking me up the way she was. I really pissed her off. Looking around the room, I saw her silk robe hanging from the back of the door. I snatched the belt from the robe and threw her in the chair she kept at her desk. I tied her hands to the side of the chair and spun her around, so she was facing me. "Now you going to calm down and listen?" Instead of responding, she sneered at me. I leaned in to kiss her but didn't get far before she kicked me in my balls.

"What the fuck Bella, you trying to kill a nigga," I barked as I stepped back and damn near fell on the bed. She had me fucked up. Shorty was doing everything to get free aside from screaming out for help. I found an extension cord in the corner and used that to tie up her feet. She wasn't about to be kicking me in the nuts every time I came close.

She got quiet and instead of cursing me out some more, began to cry. "Sire let me go. You don't care about me. You can't keep me tied to the chair forever. It's morning and Jael will be awake soon. I have to take care of my baby, and I don't want her to see me like this, I know you don't either." I ran my hand over my curls, fuck, she was right. I should have woken her ass up last night with some dick, then made her listen to me. Now shit was all the way out of control. I paced for a minute, thinking shit through before picking up my phone.

I hit Amira's name and waited for her to pick up. "What big head, it's early as fuck, and I already had to curse out ya baby mama. Talking about bring Tayari home at three in the morning. That egg head ass bitch must be snorting coke." I damn near choked trying not to laugh at my sister's antics.

"Yo get up and come meet me at this address fast. Leave Tay wit ma. I need a favor. And I already know it's going to cost me. Before you say no, you get to meet her," I said, referring to Bella.

"Say no more; I'm on the way." She hung up fast as hell as I pulled up my Bank of America app and transferred more money. After sharing my location with Amira, I sat at the end of the bed to wait.

"Bells, you still mad at a nigga?" I asked, hoping she would show me she still fucked wit me on some level. Instead, she continued staring at the floor instead of me, tears dripping from her face. After what seemed like forever, my sister hit me up telling me she was outside.

ARABELLA

$\mathcal{I}$ watched as a pretty brown skin girl followed Sire into my bedroom. I could tell she was his sister because she had those same honey colored eyes him and his brother had. She was dressed casually in a pair of grey joggers and a white t-shirt that had Favorite in grey letters. The shirt was the baby doll type and showed off her flat stomach and a shiny belly ring. She didn't have on any makeup, and her hair was pulled up in a knot on the top of her head. Her mouth was parted slightly in shock when she saw how her crazy ass brother had me tied the fuck up.

"Umm Sire, when you said I could come meet the girl you are in love with I didn't know she would be tied to a fucking chair. What are you doing?"

He didn't look remorseful at all, just shrugged and offered a sly grin. "Shit she wouldn't talk to me, what the fuck else was I supposed to do?"

"Maybe give her some space nigga. What the fuck you do to her anyway? It must be bad if you had to be doing all of this. And what the hell happened to your face. You're bleeding and scratched the fuck up. I would expect this from Cahir, hell even

Remee, but not you." She moved in my direction, and I felt my cheeks turn red. I was still in my sleep clothes, and I knew my hair had to be all over my head. I fought against my restraints, but of course I couldn't move. Grunting in frustration, I let my head fall back for a moment.

"Hi, Bella right?" His sister was in front of me now, crouching down like she was talking to a puppy or small child. I was going to fuck Sire up as soon as he let me go. Slowly I nodded, confirming who I was. "I'm Amira, and I'm so sorry my brother has lost his fucking mind and tied you to a chair. Hopefully we can see each other again under better circumstances. I own a salon on East Ave, Mira's Magic. Come get your hair done anytime you want. It's on me, well really it's on him because it looks like he owes you." She gave me a genuine smile, and despite the situation, I knew I would like her.

"Ok, enough of the fucking meet and greet. I ain't call you over here for all of that. I need you to babysit her daughter, Jael. She is a good kid, and I just need you to hang out with her for the day while Bella and I sort some shit out. Was he fucking kidding me, I knew he wasn't sending my daughter with no stranger? His sister seemed nice, but Jael was my baby, and I couldn't take any chances. I didn't just send her with random people, especially after what I went through.

Before I could protest, his sister stepped in. "I don't even know her Sire, why don't I just watch the baby here for a few hours while you and her mom talk." I mouthed thank you, and she winked at me. I hoped whatever the fuck Sire was doing would be over soon, and I could get back to my regular life, even if it did mean me crying myself silly over him for the rest of the day. "It was nice to meet you, Bella. I hope to see you soon." She followed Sire out of my bedroom, and a little while later I heard Jael's excited shrieks when she realized Sire was there. I swear she loved his ass, what a traitor. If I could have crossed my arms and pouted, I would have, but all my shit was tied the fuck up.

Before long he was back, looking sexy as fuck even though I hated his ass. All he had on was his jeans, boxers and a wife-beater. I could see the tattoos on his thick ass arms, and I felt my pussy get wet. That hoe wasn't no help, I swear. She never was when it came to Sire. He pulled me with him as he sat on the edge of the bed. Slowly he untied my wrists and ran his hands over the lines the robe left. "I'm sorry Bella, but you won't let me talk to you, and I at least need to do that, I can't just let you walk away from me."

"Sire, why do you even care? You have a woman, shit a whole family. You don't need to be bothered with me." I hated that I was feeling sad again; his lying ass wasn't even worth my tears.

"I care because I love you. Look I know me having a kid and a girl looks more than fucked up. But she ain't got nothing to do with you. If I hadn't lost touch with you, I never would have fucked with Shay. And no, I don't regret my daughter, but her mama is a different story. I settled for who was there, not who I wanted. I wanted you. I don't even feel like I'm explaining this shit so you can understand. When I saw you that night in BK, I felt like God finally answered my prayer. And honestly, I wasn't willing to lose you again for anything. So, I didn't tell you about my situation. Now, my daughter, I planned on telling you about her soon and had you asked if I had kids, I would have never lied. I ain't even one of those dudes. My shorty is my fucking heart. I was just so happy to be in your life; I fucked up. But Bells, I can't let you go. You are mine."

"So, you ready to leave her then?" I asked, holding my breath as I waited for a response. Not like that shit should have mattered, he had cut me too deep. I wasn't sure I could forgive him even if he assured me, he was walking away. He sat there silent with his head in his hands, and I knew that he wasn't leaving Shay for me. I tried not to cry in front of him, but I couldn't help the tears, it was like they had a mind of their own.

"Ma look, shit is complicated, and I can't just walk away. But I want to and eventually, I will."

I held up my hand, stopping him from saying shit else. "Please, don't say another word. I heard you out, and now you can finish untying me and leave. I respect what you are saying, and I accept your apology if that is what this is. But I have no plans on being your side chick, so this is where we have to say goodbye. It's bad enough you already turned me into one without my knowledge, but now I know better. I'm sure your girl doesn't deserve to be cheated on." He snorted and then sighed. I could see him giving up by the way his shoulders drooped when he leaned over to untie my legs. I immediately jumped up, only to have my legs give out from under me because my feet had fallen asleep.

"I got you," he said as he wrapped his arms around me, catching my body before it hit the ground. "Bella, I always got you," he said as he buried his face in my neck. I felt his warm lips as they trailed kisses along my collar bone. I weakly tried to push him away, but my hands ended up settling on his chest. "I love you Bells, please don't leave me," he pleaded in between his kisses. His hands found their way up my silk sleep shirt, and I shivered once he touched my bare skin. "Just give me one more chance," he whispered in my ear. He backed me against the wall, and his hands were caressing my breasts, causing me to moan in pleasure instead of cursing him out.

Somehow my tiny sleep shorts ended up on the ground, and his jeans became unzipped. I told myself over and over again it was just one last time and I meant it. I held my breath in anticipation, my juices sliding down my legs. Instead of entering me, he spun me around and shoved me against the wall. "This my pussy?" he asked as he forced his way inside. I couldn't even focus the way he was beating up my walls. It seemed like every time we had sex before he was holding back because today, he had my pussy ready to run away. I was trying to climb up the wall to give myself some relief, but he wasn't having that shit.

I tried to remember my daughter and his sister was in the other room and not scream too loud, but when he pulled all the way out and left the head on my clit, I lost it. Throwing my ass on him, I was begging loud as fuck for him to put it back in. Hearing him snicker I wanted to throat punch him, but that wasn't going to help me get the dick. Finally, he gave me what I wanted. His strokes were slow and steady this time, causing my pussy to spring a leak. "Damn you wet as fuck girl." He started pulling my hair, and as soon as my neck became exposed, he bit me.

Bracing myself on the wall, I popped my pussy as hard as I could chasing the feeling of pure bliss. "Please don't stop," I panted as my body tensed up. I knew I was about to cum, and I was tired of holding back. "Damn," I whispered as my body shook and I creamed all over his dick.

"You better not fucking run Bella," he demanded as he gripped my ass and went deeper. I was sniffling by then, wishing I had kept my pussy to myself. "I'm about to nut," he said before I felt him spill his seeds inside of me.

"What the hell is wrong with you Sire; why you didn't use a condom?" I snapped, cutting my eyes his way as I pushed him off of me. "You have a woman, and now I have to go get checked because I have no idea who she is fucking. I know you be sexing her, and God knows who else." He looked hurt, but what the fuck did he expect. "It's time for you to go. What just happened doesn't mean anything. It was a mistake, nothing concerning me and you has changed." I ran in the bathroom to wash off. I heard him come in and run the water in the sink, and I knew he was doing the same while I was in the shower. I would stay in here all day if I could, but I had to go and get Jael from his people. I felt so fucking stupid.

By the time I came out, he had put his dick up and was sitting on my desk chair looking pitiful. As soon as he saw me, he stood up and opened the bedroom door. I followed only to be met with his sister's grinning face. Her and Jael were in the living room with Barbies everywhere. "Mommy look at how pretty my hair is, and my nails. I have sparkles." Jael was twirling around so fast I could barely see the two French braids she had going down her back with pretty pink bows on the ends.

"Wow baby that is so pretty, can you tell Miss Amira thank you before she leaves."

She stopped suddenly and looked at all of us, her eyes wide and a frown on her face. "I don't want her to leave. Auntie Amira is the funnest. She made me pancakes with chocolate chips and did my hair and painted my nails. And when we played Barbies, she made up silly voices. No, she can't leave." She ran over to Amira and wrapped her arms around her leg.

Lord, I should have never agreed to allow his sister to keep her. "Baby, she can't stay she has her own things to go and do. Maybe you will see her again. Now, remember to say thank you, and say goodbye to Sire too. You have to go and get your stuff to go to your God mommy's. I have to get to work."

"Thank you," my baby mumbled looking crushed. Wait until she noticed that Sire wasn't coming around anymore. Her tiny heart would really be crushed then. I knew better than to allow a man around my kid. I fucked up, and I couldn't even be mad at him for that one.

"Yo Bella don't do that shit ma. You know I care about Jael, and I'm not just about to disappear out her life. Yours either but you can get ya space for now." He went to pick up Jael and promise her a trip somewhere. All I know is my daughter was giggling and hugging him like he was her daddy, and even though he played the shit out of me, I still wished he was.

"Jael, be good for your mommy, and I promise to come visit

soon. We can have a movie night, and we will make mommy watch with us. I know how to make caramel popcorn." Jael left Sire's arms and hugged Amira. His sister must have been special to gain her love that fast. I mouthed thank you to her as they left.

"Girl, you better come and get your hair done. I left my card on the counter." She reached over and hugged me before she damn near drug her brother out the door. She seemed really sweet, and I wondered if she liked his girlfriend.

* * *

NOT SEEING SIRE HAS BEEN HARD, ESPECIALLY SINCE HE CALLS ME at least ten times a day, but I knew it was for the best. Even if I had spent the past two weeks crying over the man who I had been imagining being my prince charming for years. I stretched and rolled over in my bed, using the pillow to hide my face from the sun that was streaming in. I hated that I was up so early on my day off. Jael was with Eternity, and I planned to eat chocolate, sip wine and read a good book. At least that was the plan until my phone rang. I didn't recognize the number, so I wasn't going to answer, but it called back two more times. It had better not be Sire playing games.

"Hello," I barked into the phone, hoping he could hear how pissed I was.

"Hello, Arabella?" the female voice on the other end asked timidly. Like she wasn't sure if she had the right number. Great, now his bitch was calling me.

"Can I help you?" I said making sure I sounded like the right one today because I was.

"Bella, it's me, Keke." I felt my stomach drop, and my heart race when she announced her name. It had been years since I heard from her and I had no idea how the fuck she got my number.

"Hey Keke, how have you been?" I wondered was my mom dying or something. I really had no idea why my sister was calling me now. When I was being raped, beaten and more she didn't give two fucks about me. Now my brain understood she was being treated just as bad as me at one point, but my heart didn't give a fuck and wanted me to curse her out and hang up.

"I wanted to ask if we could meet up. It's important. I know you probably don't want anything to do with me and I get it. But I'm pregnant and I really just need to talk to you. I swear I won't take up much of your time." Hearing she was pregnant softened me up a little. I was going to be an aunt, and I cared about my unborn niece or nephew because that was the kind of person I am.

"Ok, I'm off today. Let's meet at the Wegmans, the one close to downtown so that we can sit outside. I will be there at noon. If you don't show up, don't call me back because I don't like my time being wasted." She agreed, and we hung up. I felt good being in control of the situation instead of her running shit. I wasn't taking shit off of anybody these days. I was over that stage of life. If I didn't know Alex was dead, I would have been worried about him following her or her telling him she was seeing me. But I knew Sire took care of his ass, so I wasn't concerned.

I went to sleep for another hour then got up and plugged in my flat irons. After I showered, brushed my teeth and moisturized my skin, I had to find something to wear. I didn't have a lot of new clothes since my job didn't pay that much and I put my baby girl first. I grabbed a cute, black off the shoulder romper I got from Fashion Nova on sale and slid my feet into a pair of gold sandals. I pulled my long hair back into a ponytail since it was hot outside. I didn't need makeup, but I still decided to do a full face. Sliding a pair of cute shades on, I was ready to go. I waited for my Uber and hoped that I was doing the right thing meeting my sister. She was always scheming on something, and

I just knew she was about to be on some bullshit. Maybe she was going to ask me for money, but I should hope not.

I pulled up and walked inside the café area. Picking up a tray, I grabbed a plate and made a salad from the salad bar. I topped it off with strawberries and apples, grabbed a Smart Water and made my way to the cashier. By that time, I noticed my sister standing by the door anxiously waiting for me. "Hey," I said as a greeting. I was happy she didn't try to hug me or anything like that because I really wasn't on that vibe wit her. "You not about to eat?" I had noticed she didn't have any food with her.

"Naw, this baby makes me sick most of the time." I shrugged and started eating my salad. I wasn't about to starve myself due to her morning sickness.

"So, what is this visit all about? I know you just didn't call for a social visit."

"I wanted to tell your little ass to stay away from Alex," she said, her voice filled with venom. I dropped my fork, and my mouth fell open in shock. Was she smoking that shit or shooting it in her veins? Like why the fuck would I contact Alex, if he wasn't already dead, I mean. I shook my head at her and got ready for whatever because clearly, this hoe had lost her fucking mind. "He is obsessed with you. He always has been since the day he entered our home. But he had me before you, and he was my first, and I know that means something to him. We are meant to be together, and I won't allow you or your brat to ruin it for us."

"Umm Keke, I think you have shit all wrong. I don't fuck with Alex, care about Alex and haven't seen him in years."

"YOU'RE LYING," she roared, standing up to hover over me and causing people to stare. "He came home and told us how he saw you, and his precious daughter that he had been looking for, for years. I could barely get him to have sex with me once you left. Every time I got pregnant, he was dragging me down to the clinic forcing me to get an abortion, because the baby wasn't

35

yours. But not this time, I'm not allowing him to kill this one, and I'm not allowing you to come in between our love again!"

I stood up, so we were face to face. "Bitch you are sick, who the fuck wants to be with the man who sexually abused you as a child? He was a pedophile! A sick man and I hope he rots in hell." I grabbed my purse, determined to leave this psycho bitch behind. But instead of allowing me to walk off, my sister ran around the table and grabbed my arm.

"What did you mean by was? Where is Alex? I haven't seen him in weeks. I thought he was with you, but now I don't think so. He wouldn't leave me for you. He was just saying that. What did you do to him?" She was sobbing and creating an even bigger scene than before. I snapped as I looked at how she was behaving over a man who abused us.

I hit her dead in her jaw, that mother fuckin face wasn't pregnant. Making sure not to hit her in the belly I beat the hell out of her. All the anger I had been holding on to came out in each blow. "My baby," she cried out, I guess hoping I would feel sorry for her.

"Fuck you and that baby," I spat as I walked away, leaving her a bloody mess. I tried to warn her earlier that today everybody had the right one, and now she knew for sure.

* * *

EVER SINCE THE RUN-IN WITH MY SISTER, I HAD BEEN FIGHTING the urge to call Sire more and more. I was on edge just thinking about her, my mom and Alex. They turned my life into a tragedy, and I wanted nothing to do with any of them. I turned onto my left side, then back to my right and let out a huge sigh. I had to work tomorrow, and here it was three a.m and my ass was still awake with a bunch of shit on my mind. I couldn't relax if I tried. When my fucked-up family wasn't taking over my thoughts, I was consumed with wondering what Sire was doing.

Was he laid up with his woman? Or with a new girl? Did he miss me?

My hands snatched my cell phone off the charger and called him like they had a mind of their own. It rang four times, but before I could press end, he answered. He sounded wide awake, and now I really wanted to know what he was up to. "Bells you good?" He said, his voice sounding excited. But I couldn't find the words to say anything, so I stayed silent. "Bella, come on ma talk to me and let me know you aight." When I opened my mouth to speak, sobs came out instead and I hung up. Turning my phone on do not disturb I cried myself to sleep.

"Mommy," a tiny voice called. I wanted to ignore it, but then I felt the finger poking me in my eye, and I knew it was past time to get up. "Come on mommy, it's morning," my baby called out in a cheerful voice. I wanted so bad to groan, but instead, I smiled at her.

"Good morning, pretty girl." She grinned and ran out of the room. Looking at my phone, I saw dozens of missed calls on my phone then abruptly they stopped at four AM. I got out of bed and started racing around when I saw the time. I had to get the bus to Eternity's then to work, so my ass was definitely running behind. "Jael," I said, calling her so she could start to get ready. Instead of a response, I was met with silence. "Jael, come on mommy has to hurry, you need to get dressed." I was literally in the bathroom brushing my teeth and yelling for her at the same time. "Fuck," I cried out as I hit my knee on the dresser trying to put on lotion and find a bra at the same time.

"Oooh mommy, you said a bad word," Jael cried out as she ran in my room trying to check me. Now she wanted to make an appearance when I been calling her for twenty damn minutes.

"Jael didn't you hear mommy calling you. We have to go," I said, trying not to allow the anxiety I was feeling come out in my tone.

37

"But mommy, I am ready," she replied, causing my head to shoot up. Sure, enough she had on a Tommy Hilfiger dress, little white ballet looking slip-on shoes and her purse Eternity got her across the front of her body. She smelled like baby lotion and toothpaste. "I told you mommy," she giggled and ran out of the room. *How the hell did she get herself dressed?* I threw the rest of my clothes on and went to get my baby breakfast except she was already at the counter eating fruit and a half of a bagel.

I spun around only to see Sire relaxing on my couch like he lived in my shit. "Nigga, seriously? Didn't I tell you don't be breaking in my crib anymore?" I hissed low trying not to alert my baby girl to how pissed off I was.

"Well don't be fucking calling me in the middle of the night crying and shit then don't answer your phone. The fuck I was supposed to do curl up and go to bed not knowing if my shorty and her little one was good or not? I ain't no sucka ass nigga ma, so I stopped what the fuck I was doing and came to make sure ya'll was good. Just finish getting ready, so I can give you a ride and then I'm out." He turned back to the TV dismissing me, I guess. As much as I didn't want to ride with him, I was going to be late otherwise.

"I'm ready."

"You not about to eat?" He looked at me crazy knowing I loved breakfast. I just shook my head no. I wanted to get this shit over with, so I could get out of his presence. He was nothing but temptation, the perfect nigga, except he belonged to someone else. We walked out together, and he put Jael in his truck. Before I could open my door, he was on me. "So that's it ma, you not fuckin wit me?" I wanted to throw myself on him, and the grey sweatpants he had on showing his print wasn't helping any.

Nudging away from him, I backed up some and closed my eyes. Although that didn't stop the smell of his cologne from invading my senses. *Stay strong.* "Yea, I told you I'm off you nigga. I don't fuck with men who are taken." I let myself in the truck while he stood there watching me like a predator. Finally, he got in and drove me to Eternity's house.

After dropping my baby off, I felt my nerves intensify now that I was alone with Sire. He side-eyed me as I crept closer to the door. I wanted to jump the fuck out his ride, but he was doing ninety on the expressway, and a bitch wouldn't have made it. "Yo, I ain't bout to fuck wit you. Stop acting like I be beating ya ass or some shit." He had the nerve to look annoyed like he wasn't the one who lied to me. I wasn't on no shit, he was.

"Whatever," I responded, rolling my eyes and folding my arms over my chest. I stayed that way until we pulled up at Burger King. Grabbing my purse, I went to get out without saying shit but decided at the last minute to at least say thank you. "I appreciate the ride Sire, thanks."

"Can I have a hug Bells?" He gave me his best puppy dog face. Shaking my head, no, my body did what it wanted because I was leaning over the console, my arms snaking around his body. For a second, I rested my face in his neck and inhaled his scent. "I don't want us to be arguing and shit Bells. Just know you got a nigga's heart. I'm not letting you go." I didn't respond. Instead, I literally jumped up out the truck. I didn't want him to see how sad I was thinking about what could have been between us.

We were busy as hell most of the day, and I was grateful for that. I didn't want to stop and think about anything to be honest. "Hey Bella, can you go and wipe the tables in the front before you go," my annoying ass manager demanded. Like he didn't see me counting out my drawer.

"Sure, Chris." I grabbed the spray bottle and a clean rag and walked from behind the counter. I groaned as soon as I saw the next customer to walk through the door was Jax. He hadn't been in much since Sire told him to leave me alone and when he did come in, he wouldn't say shit to me. But I had a feeling today was going to be different.

"Hey girl you look sexy as fuck today." He licked his lips and looked at me like I was on the menu, causing my skin to crawl.

"What do you want," I hissed. Not giving a fuck about being professional at that moment. It was a fast-food job, and I didn't get paid enough to fake being nice to this annoying mother-fucker. He was damn near stalking me at this point.

Jax moved closer and lightly grabbed my hand. "Ma, I just wanted to apologize for allowing you to get mixed up with my boy, knowing he had a woman at home. I mean I ain't that kind of dude to be spreading rumors and shit. But now that you know Sire don't really fuck wit you, you can come and join my team." I couldn't even find words for this dummy. Partially because what he said was true and that shit hurt. But also, because what kind of grown ass man ran behind some pussy his homie already had.

"What the fuck is going on here," I heard Sire's voice say, causing my head to shoot up. His face was twisted up in a look of anger, and his hand was at his waist. That was when I realized Jax was still holding my hand.

CAHIR

I stood in the corner of Club Remi` with my hood up and my back against the wall. "Ransom, would you like a table upstairs," one of the waitresses asked. Her name was Lisa. She was a good little worker, and she never tried to fuck wit me. I was pretty sure her ass was scared of me, as she should have been.

"Naw, I'm good right here," I lifted the bottle of Henny showing her I didn't need a drink. I hoped she got the fucking hint and left me alone. She stepped back at the look on my face and damn near ran the other way. I continued to stand there, watching Eternity. I could tell by her movements and slight facial expressions she hated working down here. But she hid it well for the customers. She glanced my way a couple of times, and I really couldn't read the look in her eyes. I knew I was on some weird shit watching her all night, but I just couldn't leave shorty alone.

"Hey baby, you want to meet me upstairs?" Deanna stood in front of me with her hand on her hip. She arched her back so her breasts would sit up more, the tiny shorts she had on were so tight I could see her pussy print. "I can get you right on my break," she pushed, smirking at me like I couldn't resist a wet mouth or pussy. There was only one female that had me on that shit, and I was currently trying to stay away from her, unsuccessfully that is.

"Move," I snapped because she was blocking my view of Eternity.

"Daddy come on, I said I was sorry about the other night."

"Bitch move," I roared and shoved her, so she was out of the way. "Do you actually work up in here or just suck and fuck niggas." She stood there looking hurt, but I didn't know for what. We never did anything more than fuck, and the way I sexed her was so degrading that this couldn't have been the thing to bruise her feelings.

"Deanna, take ya ass back to work before you don't have a job," Natalie said as she walked up on us. I saw Deanna glare at Eternity before stomping off. I swear she better not fuck wit her. Natalie stood next to me, her eyes following my line of sight. "Really Cahir, what the fuck. You ruined her, just like I knew you would, and what you back to do more damage? Or just fuck with her head?"

"Yo, who the fuck is you talking to."

"Nigga, I'm talking to you. I don't fuck you and even though I know you crazy, I ain't scared of you. Cahir, that girl liked you. I told you Eternity was a good one and to just leave her alone. You fucked with her job, her heart and her life. These hoes in here giving her hell because they think ya'll on something. She is losing money and you over here watching her like an animal ready to attack." Natalie snapped on my ass, then walked away.

I didn't want to think about the shit she said, but she was right. I could see that baby girl was suffering, and it had me feeling some kind of way. Instead of leaving, I stayed. Every time I saw some nigga order a drink from her, I felt myself getting heated. My fists clenched as some light skin nigga lingered at the bar trying to hold a conversation with Eternity until she politely turned him down. He hadn't even made it five feet before some other cat was in her face grinning and shit. Losing my patience for these sucka ass niggas, I walked over and pulled out a stack. "Yo, I need another bottle," I said, cutting old boy off in the middle of his sentence.

"Ransom, you can wait," she snapped as she went back to talking with her customer.

"Damn baby girl, I like a girl with an attitude. You need to let me take you home tonight, and you can show me how mean you can get." This dude had the nerve to laugh like a bitch after. I expected her to straight shut this nigga down, but instead, she smiled like she was considering it.

"Naw, she ain't going home with no one tonight. It's time for you to move the fuck around." I wanted a reason to blast this nigga, but he backed away with his hands up before I could even reach for my nine.

"What the fuck, Cahir," she hissed. I didn't respond, just threw the money down in front of her and went to go and find Remee. I didn't even want another drink, that bread was my way of helping her out since I fucked up her funds. I stumbled upstairs to his office and bust through the door.

"Get the fuck out," he said, not even looking up. Ever since he decided to let Rumor go, his attitude has been the worst. Even I didn't want to be around this nigga. "Since you don't know how to leave when I tell you what the fuck you want?"

"You need to man up and get the fuck out your feelings. I want you to put Eternity back in the VIP sections. Those niggas thirsty as fuck at the bar. I wouldn't even be mad if you fired her. I don't want these motherfuckers looking at her."

He lifted his head then and stared at me before he chuckled to himself. "Cahir, she is working the bar, unless she quits. Now if you want to make decisions on people's positions and shit, open ya own fucking club. Maybe you need to man up and realize you like shorty. Now leave me the fuck alone." He picked up the bottle of Patron he had on the desk and went back to drinking.

"Fuck you," I said as I slammed his door.

* * *

TWO WEEKS LATER AND I WAS STILL SHOWING UP TO MY COUSIN'S club keeping my eyes on shorty. I was starting to feel like a stalker, and me following her home didn't help. I parked a few spaces away from her when she pulled up to her townhouse. Everything in me wanted to knock on the door and apologize, but my pride wouldn't let me. And even if I got past that, I pushed shorty away for a reason. I sat there watching the clock, telling myself to pull away, but I couldn't. I needed to see her, make sure she was ok.

Slowly I made my way from the car to her door, I used a tool to unlock the door, and I quietly closed it behind me. Good thing I knew how to move in silence, I couldn't count the number of nigga's I had put to sleep after I was up and through their crib. It was late as fuck and Eternity just worked a long shift, but as I crept up the stairs, I heard her voice. I stopped in the hallway and hoped for her sake she wasn't talking to no nigga.

"Bella, I wasn't in love. I was in like. I really liked him, and he turned on me. Yes, I feel hurt, but I also feel stupid. I'm not even sure what I was doing fucking with him. Clearly, he wasn't settling down with any female. I wasn't even trying to change him. I just enjoyed whatever we had. He made me happy." Hearing her say that shit had my stomach in knots. I never wanted to hurt her, and as much as she denied loving the kid, her voice said it all.

I heard Bella snort and realized they were on speaker phone. "Girl you loved his ass, I can tell." I nodded, agreeing even though no one could see me.

"I mean it was too soon for love, but I was for sure feeling some shit I never felt before. I mean it was definitely never going anywhere, he didn't like kids. My son will always come first. It was just when he was with me, I felt, special." She sighed, and I could imagine her laying on her stomach, her chin propped up on her hand and a pout on her face. She would watch TV that way when I would come through and chill. I missed spending time with her, more than just fucking, but just being in her presence. She always had me spending nights with her not doing anything but cuddling like a bitch.

"Umm, girl fuck that creepy ass nigga. He looks like he will murder you in ya sleep. And fuck him for not appreciating my friend. You're a bad ass chick, a great mom and if he can't see that you don't need him. Shit all those niggas in your DM, you better give one of them a chance. No sense in waiting for a nigga who don't want to be kept and who clearly didn't give damn about you at all." I bawled up my fists at what Sire's broke shorty said. She was right about Eternity being a bad ass chick. But she took it too far encouraging her to fuck with other dudes. If I was a social media ass type of nigga, I would be on her page seeing who was trying to get with shorty. I knew I was on some fuckboy shit. I didn't want her but didn't want anyone else to have her either. I never cared about shit, and I was going to do whatever the hell I wanted. It ain't have to make sense to anyone but me. I sat on the top step and leaned against the wall. I had to see who the fuck Bella thought baby girl was about to slide on to next. I just had to wait for Tee to fall asleep.

I listened as she chatted to her homegirl for another forty minutes. Sire had his work cut out for him if he was getting her back. And me and him were going to have a talk about his run-in with Jax. That nigga violated, but Sire pistol-whipping him in Burger King wasn't on my list of smart shit to do. Finally, they hung up, and I listened to shorty tossing and turning for a while. Once her breathing evened out, I walked into her room.

She had fallen asleep on her stomach, her phone next to her. She ain't have on shit but a little pink tank top and a pair of black silk panties. I felt my dick brick up, and I had to remind myself I had broke in her shit.

I couldn't help but touch her. Lightly, I let my hand caress her cheek. This was the shit I was talking about, shorty had me weak as fuck. Angry with myself, I snatched the phone and set on her bench. She didn't keep a lock on her shit, so I hit the IG app and went to her messages. Scrolling through each message, I couldn't believe the number of niggas that was hitting her up. These motherfucka's was offering her everything from dick to new cars. I had never felt the rage I was feeling now over any female. This shit had my head fucked up. A new message popped up from this nigga named Slim. I knew him from the hood. He sold shake outside the corner store on Clifford and North. Ole boy was calling Eternity all kinds of bitches and shit because she turned his ass down. What the fuck was wrong with this cat, if a female doesn't want you move the fuck around. Too bad for him, he got mad at the wrong one.

I threw shorty's phone on the bed and let my gaze linger on her for a few more minutes. I crept out and made sure her shit was locked. Hopping in my whip, I peeled the fuck out and went straight to the store Slim hung out at. Sure, enough his ass was outside leaned up against the brick wall, smoking a cigarette with his phone in his hand.

"Yo Slim," I called out as I approached him, only for his hoe ass to look up and grin.

"Damn Ransom, what's up my dude. You ready to put a real one on the team?"

"Nigga, I ain't here to talk about your fucking fantasies. You been hitting up a chick named Eternity in her DM?"

"Yea, shorty got a fat ass. Don't want to give me the pussy yet, but she will." I swear he licked his lips and I knew he was

46

imagining fucking Eternity. I felt like I was about to lose my fucking mind.

"Bitch, you been hitting up my girl in her fucking DM." His eyes got wide as fuck. I don't know if it was from what I revealed or from the Ruger SR that was pointed at his chest. "I would say let this be a lesson, but there won't be a next time for sure." I pulled the trigger three times, blasting his face off. "Disrespectful motherfucker," I spat before I walked away.

ETERNITY

$\mathcal{I}$ looked in the mirror and tried to smile. I told myself I didn't even know Cahir like that to feel this hurt. But shit I was. I had never met a man like him, and even though from jump it felt like we never had a chance, I really wanted him. The way he came to my job every night lately, just watching me had me ready to request a transfer or find a new career. The shit made no sense. He was the one who told me he didn't want to fuck with me. I eyed the stack of money sitting on my dresser. It was the same money Cahir tipped me the other day. I wanted to give it back, maybe throw it in his face, but I swallowed my pride since I could use it. After going back and forth on the situation, I finally came to the conclusion his ass owed me since he fucked up my job. A job I loved, that had become one I tolerated.

My new manager at the bar was a far cry from Natalie. I mean she did her job, but I was pretty sure she had been fucked by Ransom and was taking it out on me. During my shifts, she made sure her petty shined through. And personally, I was sick of it. That was why I called off last night and again today. I was taking a me day, well a me and Cassian day. I was about to spoil my baby some. We both needed it. "I'm ready mommy," he got out in between bouncing his way into my room. My baby was cute in his blue jeans, white, green and yellow Polo shirt and wheat Timbs. "I hope they have the sneakers I want." He said with a grin. Shit, I did too, I wasn't standing in line for Jordan's for a damn preschooler, but I would buy my baby the black and yellow 12's he desired if they were available in his size.

"I hope so too. Now let's go," I said, sliding the cash into my MK bag. We drove to the bigger mall in Victor so we could have lunch at P.F. Changs after. It was my favorite. Footlocker was jumping, and I rolled my eyes at all the niggas calling out to me. I hated shit like that, especially when I was with my son. I had on a True Religion sweatsuit. It wasn't like I was out here half-naked. Yea my mid-drift was showing, but that shouldn't scream looking for some average ass nigga to press up on me. Or maybe it did.

"Excuse me I need a pair of sneakers," I called out to the overwhelmed sales associate. He held up his finger to say one minute. In the meantime, I grabbed Cassian some Nike, Jordan and Adidas outfits. I had filled two of the mesh shopping bags they provided by the time he finally made it over to me. "Can I have the blue Foamposites, red Airmaxes, those two Nike slides and the new Jordan's, all in a size twelve and the Uggs furry slides in pink and red size six."

"We don't have the Jordan's in that size, they are sold out. Meet me at the front for the rest unless you want to try them on." His voice was monotone, and he sounded like he hated his job. That shit wasn't my problem though. Before I could ask him to call another location for the sneakers I really wanted, he walked away.

"It's ok mommy. I can get yellow sneakers next time." My son slipped his hand in mine and smiled up at me.

That was why I didn't mind going hard for mine. He was a good kid and had already been through enough. I don't know if he remembered the way his father used to beat me in front of him. I prayed he was too young, but sometimes I wondered. He was way to overprotective of me to be so young. "We can look online baby I will find them." I walked to the register and stood there talking to my son as I waited. During the process of checking out, I wandered to look at the socks they kept nearby.

"Ok ma'am your all set," the cashier said. He had a smirk on his face as he handed me my bags.

"I didn't pay yet." I stood patiently waiting on my total. I knew they were busy, but damn he was about to let me walk out with at least a thousand dollars worth of shit.

"It was already paid for," he said, looking at someone behind me and holding out a receipt. It would be him. I was seriously feeling stalked now. How the fuck was he in the mall following me. Paying for my shit. Snatching the receipt and the last of my bags I stomped over to Cahir.

"What the fuck Ransom. I don't want your help or your money. I can pay for my own shit. You don't fuck wit me, and I ain't no charity case. All I want you to do is leave me the hell alone." It seemed like the entire store had stopped to look at us, and I could feel my face getting flushed in embarrassment. I reminded myself that my son was with me, so I took a deep breath, and got ready to try again, only calmer. Cahir was just standing there. His eyes blank like I wasn't even talking to him.

"Eh yo shorty, I paid for ya shit ma, not him. My bad, I meant to catch you before you left so I could get your number and we could chill." My head spun around to see some dude standing there, a lopsided grin on his face. He was handsome. I couldn't deny that, his waves were spinning, and his hazel eyes most likely got him a gaggle of bitches. Too bad the only man who turned me on these days didn't fuck wit me. And now I had embarrassed myself in front of him. I let the fact sink in, that I was cussing Ransom out in front of all these people, for nothing.

I would deal with the unwanted nigga behind me in a second. "My bad, I'm sorry, the cashier looked in this direction, and I saw you, and I just assumed." His eyes had changed, and instead of the blank look, there was rage. Those mahfuckers seemed like they were on fire. He didn't respond, just looked beyond me at old boy who bought my shit. Suddenly he snatched my wrist, causing a chill to run through my body. I missed his touch, even though a part of me hated him, the rest of me longed for him. He grabbed the receipt from my hand and let me go. He scanned it and shook his head like he was holding a conversation with himself.

"Son what's good," Sire said as he walked up to us. I silently groaned, not one but two McKenzie's in a public space was sure to bring even more attention to whatever the fuck was going on. "Hey Cassian, you alright little man," he said giving my son a pound. He nodded at me, and I waved.

"Hi Sire," he called out cheerfully, and I realized my son must spent time around him when he was with Bella. Cassian wasn't the friendliest kid, so Sire must be a good guy to get him to speak. Even though Sire lied to my friend, I did believe he cared about her. "I'm getting new sneakers, but not the ones I wanted. They didn't have the new Jordan's in my size," Cassian contiued, causing Cahir to look down.

"What size," he said, speaking for the first time.

"A twelve," he responded, and Cahir nodded his head.

"Cool, I got you. Why don't you go with Sire for a minute so I can talk to your mommy?" Before I could object, Cassian was skipping over to Sire and holding a whole animated conversation. Cahir walked past me to mister Romeo, who was still waiting for my attention. "Eh yo, my nigga, get this bread." He reached in his pocket and handed him at least double what he spent. "You buying her shit, that's dead. You thought you were going to drop a little nine hunnit dollars and she was going to hand you the pussy? You a cornball ass nigga for that." I could see by the look on this dude's face that he really did think I was going to fuck him for dropping some money, money that I didn't ask him to spend, to begin with. "The fuck you still standing here for, take ya money and get the fuck on," Cahir barked causing him to take the money and leave.

"I can pay you back, I want to pay you back. Let me just grab the money out of my purse." He gave me a look that could freeze hell, causing my hand to pause.

"I don't want your bread shorty."

"I wasn't going to fuck him," I blurted out. I have no clue why I said that shit.

He looked at me, his face had this look on it I had never seen. It was almost loving, but only there for a moment. "Yea I know," he said before walking away.

* * *

I couldn't get past the look on Cahir's face yesterday in the mall. I barely slept last night because I wanted him to come and look at me that way again. Then I wanted him to fuck me silly. I should have never gotten involved with him. This nigga was like crack, exclusive crack that I couldn't get, but I craved. Grabbing my iPhone, I pulled up google to see if you could be addicted to dick. Laughing at my damn self, I threw the phone on my bed and got up to brush my teeth and wash my face.

"Hey Cass, you want pancakes?" I asked my son as he watched cartoons.

"Yes please," he responded grinning at the thought of his favorites. "Mommy, that man likes you," he said, causing me to drop an egg on the floor.

"What man," I asked, holding my breath waiting to hear his response.

"The one who is getting my sneakers. I could tell mommy."

"You know he isn't going to get your sneakers baby. He was

just being nice. And I'm pretty sure he doesn't like mommy. Now go watch your cartoons and stay out of my business." He giggled at the last part like I said something funny and went back to the TV. I continued making breakfast, but my mind kept running back to him. Did Cahir like me? Shit, he was so hard to read, to understand. And he straight told me he didn't like me, basically said my pussy was trash.

My doorbell rang, causing me to snap out of my thoughts. I damn near raced to the door wondering was it Cahir, I didn't know what I would say if it was. Snatching the door open I made sure I had my attitude in place in case he stopped by with some more fuck boy shit. Seeing my mother and sister on the other side of the door, I wanted to slam it in their faces. What the hell did they want?

"Hey Eternity," my mother sang out in greeting as she damn near shoved me down while squeezing herself into my house. "You haven't been to family dinner in a few months, so I came to check on you," she said, causing me to roll my eyes. What fucking family? I barely spoke to her, let alone came around. My older sister Megan didn't say shit to me, just followed our mother. That bitch was so fucking rude, and I swear I couldn't stand her raggedy ass. As I went to close the door, it was damn near flung back open by some man I had never seen before.

"That's my man, Tyree. Tyree, this is my sister Eternity." My sister made the introduction like I was bothering her or something. I was surprised this bitch could get a man, even a low-quality one like this nigga. It wasn't because she was ugly, because she wasn't. Outside my sister was cute, big booty, pretty face. But her insides were rotten. That bitch had a nasty attitude since the day I was born. Her 'man' stood there eye-fucking me. I only had on some boy shorts and a cami since I wasn't expecting company. But this nigga made me want to run and find some clothes, a blanket, anything to cover up.

"Umm give me a minute to go and find something to put on,

I didn't know you were stopping by. You can have a seat, I guess." I turned to go upstairs and was stopped at the sound of Tyree's voice.

"Shit you look fine with what you got on to me," he sneered causing me to shudder.

I was annoyed that my mother chose today to stop by and brought Megan with her. I didn't fuck with my sister period. She had done some grimy shit to me in the past, including fucking Cassian's father when I was in the hospital giving birth. If she knew what I knew, she could have had his crazy ass. My mother usually only came around when she wanted something, so I was sure today wasn't any different.

I pulled on a pair of black sweats from PINK and a matching hoodie. Stopping to put my hair up into a bun, I dropped the brush as I heard loud voices from downstairs. I was already racing down the stairs when I heard what sounded like my son crying. "What the fuck is the problem?" I snapped as I flew into the living room. My eyes bucked when I saw Cassian run to Cahir, his face stained with tears. Cahir picked him up and checked him over before he ran his hand over his curls in a loving manner.

Tyree stood there with a scowl on his face, holding my remote control in his hand. I noticed he had got comfortable in the five minutes I had been gone. Took off his sneakers and his t-shirt and was walking around with some baller shorts and a wife-beater. What the fuck! Cahir came and handed me my son. He gave me a disappointed look. And even though I knew what he thought was happening wasn't even it, I felt like shit.

"You put ya fucking hands on him?" Cahir said as he swung on Tyree. He hit him three times in a row, causing a tooth to fly out of his mouth and blood to start leaking from his face. "Get the fuck out," Ransom said calm as hell. Megan ran up to Tyree using his t-shirt to soak up the blood. "You lucky lil man is here because that is the only thing that saved your life."

"What is wrong with you, he didn't even do anything to the little brat. He should learn when an adult speaks to shut the fuck up and listen." My sister screeched as she helped her man.

"Megan, he is your nephew what the fuck is wrong with you. You can all leave, get the fuck out. I'm sure your only here to ask for money anyway, and I ain't got it. Now leave before I fuck you up in front of my son." I walked to the front door and snatched it opened.

"Baby, you know she didn't mean it like that," my mom tried as she stopped near me before leaving. She raised her hand to rub Cassian's back, but I smacked that shit down.

"Bitch you're his grandmother, and you just sat back and allowed whatever the fuck was happening to go down. I mean it this time, don't fucking come back here. She gave me a dirty look before leaving. I closed the door and sank against the wall. "You ok baby?" I asked Cass as he looked up at me.

"Yes, auntie's friend was mean. He wanted to change the channel, and I told him no I was watching my show. He pushed me down and took the remote. But its ok, Cahir saved me." He looked over at Cahir with adoration in his eyes. Shit, I had forgotten that nigga was even here. Why the fuck was he here?

"Thank you," I said sincerity in my voice. I realized I was shaking, I didn't know if it was from fear of what happened to my son, or anger for the same reason.

"You ok," he said as he stepped closer to me. I nodded yes. "Aight, I just stopped by to drop those sneakers off for little man." He pointed to the Footlocker bags on the table. I wondered what he bought him because there was more than one bag. Cassian wiggled to get out of my arms and ran over to the table. He started pulling out Jordan box after box along with some matching tracksuits.

"Here mommy, these are not my size," Cassian said, running over with the 12's in my size. "Thank you, Cahir," my son said as he dapped him up. My baby was so excited he just ran back to his pile of stuff.

"You didn't have to," I started to say before he cut me off.

"I know." He said, cocky as fuck like always. He turned to leave, but I grabbed his arm. He looked down at me like I was burning his skin or some shit.

"You don't have to leave."

"Shorty ain't nothing changed. I made a promise to lil man, and I always keep my word. Ya'll be good."

REMEE

"*D*addy, can you buy me a puppy," Laya said from the backseat of my Range. Her pretty eyes sparkled, and she smiled at me, knowing I would have given her the fucking world.

"What kind of puppy you want baby girl?"

"No fucking puppy is the one she wants! I wish the hell you would A'Remee. I will ensure it runs away the first day at my house. I don't do dogs period, and with work and school, I don't have time for pets." Rumor glared at me from the passenger seat. Shit had been rough lately, and just getting her to agree that Laya needed to be with both of us once she left the hospital had been hell. I knew I fucked up, gave up on her too fast, and a bunch of other shit. She probably would have been able to tough out whatever this shit was about to amount to with Jayda. But a nigga really didn't know what the fuck to do at the time.

"Watch the attitude when it comes to my shorty, real talk. You need to stop working that ghetto ass job anyway. It ain't like you need it. Every fucking time I come up there it looks like a strip club minus the poles." A look of disbelief then a roll of her eyes and then nothing, silence. The same shit she been on.

"Daddy gonna get you a puppy at grandma's house. We can go and pick it out this weekend." I smiled when my baby girl did too. She was jumping around in her seat, most likely planning all the shit she wanted her puppy to have. I hoped my mom didn't fuck me up when she found out about her newest room-mate. When we pulled up at my house, I could see Rumor's body stiffen. She damn near jumped out as she went to grab her suitcase from the back. Of course, shorty slammed my trunk as she went to the door.

"Mommy needs a nap," Laya tried to whisper as I picked her up out the back and walked to the house. I wanted to agree, but right now Ru looked like she would slice my throat, so I just chuckled.

"Come on Ru, shit don't have to be this fucking bad between us. At the end of the day we still love each other, just because we're not together doesn't mean we forget all we had."

"Remee, please shut the fuck up and tell me what guest room I can sleep in." I looked at her crazy. She always slept in my room, in my bed. Hell, she had a toothbrush in the bathroom.

"I will just figure it out myself. I'm going to lay down with Laya for a nap, I'm tired. Not that I have to explain to you." I kissed my daughter on her forehead and handed her over to her scorned mother.

Since it was still early in the day, I figured I would go handle some shit that was on my list of things to do. The first one is seeing what conditions this bitch had my son living in. I eyed the envelope with the confirmed DNA results in it and the one next to it with the shit my lawyer had drawn up. Grabbing up both I texted one of my workers, Jay, to make sure everything was ready. The whole drive to Clifford Ave, I was stressed. I didn't even want to look at this baby and damn sure didn't want to see his mama. Parking in the driveway I frowned at the dope boys hanging out on the front steps. "Ya'll niggas get the fuck from round here," I barked causing them all to scatter.

Jayda was already standing in the doorway like she was waiting on me to come over. She had on some tight ass shorts, and a tiny cropped shirt. Her body bounced the fuck back but looking at shorty caused my dick to shrivel into my body. I'm pretty sure that wasn't the effect she was looking for. "Hey baby daddy," she squealed as I walked up. She tried to hug me, but I brushed her off.

"Sup," I said as I sidestepped her and entered the living room. I scanned the house and was pleased. Even though it was in the hood, this shit was spotless. My son was in some little swing shit, with a little red footie suit. He looked fresh, and I was thankful for that. Two small kids sat on the couch, watching TV.

"Ajay, Savannah said hello to Javani's dad." The little girl grinned at me and waved, but the little boy just stared. Little nigga looked like he had a problem wit me. I walked over to speak to the kids and handed them both a hundred-dollar bill. "Aww babe you're so sweet," Janay cooed as she moved to stand next to me. "I'm so glad you finally came to visit. You want me to cook something for you?"

"I ain't come over here for all of that, and you know it. We need to sit down and talk." She shrugged, rolled her eyes and led the way to the kitchen. "You gave the lawyer your account info?"

"I had to go and open a bank account, but yes, I gave it to him. I don't understand why the fuck you just can't give me cash." She whined.

"What kind of grown ass woman don't have a fucking bank account? Man, I swear I want to kill my damn self for fucking you." I drug my hand over my face, this was the person who would be raising my son. And that thought was a scary one. "Let's just get this shit over with. I bought you a house, it's furnished, a new vehicle that is currently parked at the house. I'm giving you three thousand dollars a month in child support. You get an extra five thousand this month to hire some help as far as cleaning, you and the kids eating out and any little things you want new for the house. That's to give you a break since you just gave birth. He has been added to my health insurance. Inside this envelope are his insurance cards, doctor's info, and all the keys to the new spot. I do not have a key to your crib. I don't give a fuck what you do in there as long as he is cool. I will call anytime I want to come and spend time with him or scoop him up. When he gets older and has school, activities and all that shit we can review amounts. Any questions?"

"Where is this house and what kind of car. Plus, I think three thousand dollars seems kind of low. How much do you give Rumor for that kid who isn't even yours? Maybe I should hire a lawyer to review this."

"Bitch, I swear you want to end up in Lake Erie, your face will be the advertisement for an episode of *Unsolved Mysteries*. Don't you ever in ya fucking life ask me how much money I give Rumor. That shit don't concern you, but just know this, she gets way more than that. Now, as for the rest, get a lawyer, I don't give a fuck. My shit is solid. Your house is in Chili, it's a new build. Shit nice as fuck. I copped you a Honda Odyssey, got TV's and shit in the back."

Shorty face had a look of horror on it. "You did fucking what? I know your whack ass people live in Pittsford, in a gated community and you got me living in Chili? That suburb is for middle-class people. I'm trying to live like I'm rich. And a van? That's a joke, right? I swear I ain't riding no fucking van."

My phone rang, and I saw Rumor's name flash across the screen. I put my hand up so Jayda would pause her temper tantrum. "Sup ma, ya'll good?"

"Rem, I'm hungry. Can you bring us some wings from Magic Wings?"

"Aight, you want hot wings or garlic parm?" I knew her ass had to be starving because I hadn't bought groceries in a minute. My fridge only had juice for chaser and bottled waters.

"Both, and fries, red velvet cheesecake and a Tahitian Treat."

"Aight, I got you. Give me like thirty minutes, and I will be home." She hung up without saying thank you, causing me to laugh. Ole mean ass, she was treating me like hell but knew I was going to get her everything she wanted.

"Yo, I got shit to do, if you don't like the van take the bus. It's simple. Let me know when you've moved in so I can bring my mom to see the baby. Until then, don't hit me up." I could have called Rumor back once I left Jayda's house, but I wanted to make it clear who would always come first in my life.

* * *

I watched A'Laya as she slept, she had on her little pink PJs with sparkly hearts. This seemed like the only time I could find peace lately was when she was with me. A few days had gone by since she came home from the hospital and Rumor spent most of that time avoiding me. Not to mention Jayda called and texted me twenty-four seven. I didn't even remember Shay annoying Sire that much when she first had Tayari. Maybe she could talk to her homegirl on proper baby mama etiquette.

There was a light knock on the door, causing me to look up. "The fuck you knocking for Rumor."

"You know why the fuck I'm knocking, we ain't on it like that anymore. I don't want to argue, I can't keep going back and forth wit you. I just came to ask for some Tylenol or something." She looked like shit, she hadn't been to get her hair done, and her braids were looking frizzy. I could see the bags under her eyes, letting me know she hadn't slept in days. I got up to go into my bathroom and get her some Tylenol. I handed her the bottle, and she mumbled thank you before leaving the room. Seeing how broken she was had me feeling some kind of way. I laid there looking at the ceiling for hours before I got up to put A'Laya in her bed. I tucked her in and turned on her night light.

I stood outside of the bedroom Rumor was in wanting to go in but not wanting to make her feel worse. Once I heard the sniffles from the other side, I said fuck it and opened the door. Neither one of us said a word, I walked over and lifted her in my arms. I carried her to my room and set her on the bed. I went to get a cold cloth for her head because I could tell she was in pain. I slipped into the bed next to her and pulled her into my arms. This was all I had been wanting, Ru close to me. She was like the air I breathed, I needed her. "Ma, you gotta stop crying if you want your head to stop hurting."

"I know," she said, turning to face the wall. I didn't push, just kissed the back of her neck as I pulled her closer. I waited until I could tell she was asleep before closing my eyes and doing the same.

The next day I woke up late as fuck. I expected to be in bed by myself, but Rumor was sitting up against the pillows with A'Laya in front of her. She was taking her braids out of her hair and watching some comedy on Netflix. "Morning ma," I said as I leaned up and kissed her. Instead of cussing me out, she just sat there.

"Morning," she replied, her voice emotionless. I guess that was better than it being hostile. That made me feel even worse about the shit I had to go and do today. I swear anytime I had to do anything pertaining to Jayda I felt guilty as fuck. I wasn't even wit Rumor, but I felt like I was cheating on my wife or some shit.

"Morning daddy, I want a kiss too," A'Laya said, side-eyeing me. I kissed my baby girl on her cheek and tickled her belly.

I got up and went into the bathroom to handle my hygiene. Once I finished showering, I threw on some grey Nike sweats and a black tee. "Aight, I will be back in a little while," I said as I sprayed on cologne.

"That's what your wearing," Rumor said as she got off the bed and walked towards me. She let her gaze rake up and down my frame, stopping at my grey sweats. She was zeroed in on my dick print, and it was like somehow, she knew I was headed to Jayda's house. "Easy access right," she said, laughing. Except that shit didn't come out as a joke.

"The fuck you on Ru?" I snatched her up and pushed her in the bathroom. A'Laya was zoned into some kids show and not paying us any attention. I pushed her up against the door and got close enough so she could feel how hard my dick was. The t-shirt she had on rode up, and I could see her red panties. I didn't give her a chance to try and get away. I pushed them to the side, slid down my sweats and pushed my way inside.

"Ahhh," she moaned as I beat her pussy up. Rumor was wet and tight as fuck like always. My phone was ringing back to back, and I knew it was either my mom or Jayda, I was supposed to be over there twenty minutes ago. But I didn't give a fuck. "Remee, please don't stop."

"Cum on this dick, this what ya ass wanted, make sure you enjoy this shit. Giving me all that fucking attitude for nothing." I felt her pussy tighten around me, and I knew I wasn't going to last much longer. I tangled my right hand in her braids and pulled her head back. Biting her neck, I felt myself ready to nut. I stayed inside of her feeling her body shudder. I held her close to me, and she laid her head on my shoulder. I didn't want to let her go. I was mad at myself because we shouldn't be doing this shit and I was mad at myself because I wanted to do this again.

"You good now, I can wear my sweats, or you still think I'm going to give the dick to someone else?"

"Bye Remee," she said, sliding down my body and walking over to the shower. I washed up and left. I knew my mother was about to fuck me up. By the time I pulled up to the house and parked I noticed my sister's car parked in the driveway and sighed. Before I could even ring the bell, the door was being opened.

"Really Remee, you send your family here and don't even

show up?" Jayda bitched as soon as I walked through the door. This visit was going wrong already, but it was worth it to get some of Rumors fire ass pussy.

"You and Ru so nasty, damn you couldn't do that shit another time. Got us over here dealing with ya thotsicle ass baby momma while you fucking. Ain't that what got you in trouble in the first place," Amira said talking shit as I walked in the living room. She was sitting next to my mother, holding my sons' tiny hand in hers. My mother gave me a look, and I knew she had a lot to say, but she was classy enough to wait until later.

I sat down next to her and kissed her on the cheek. "Wassup ma, my bad, I got caught up at the last minute."

"Umm hmm," she said her lips turned up into a smirk. "You want him," she said trying to hand me the baby. I damn near jumped the fuck off the couch.

"Naw, I'm good." Both her and my sister gave me a shocked look. I knew they were confused. When A'Laya was a baby I rarely let anyone hold her when I was around. She was in my arms damn near the whole day. I just couldn't bring myself to get attached to my son yet. I was trying, but every time I was around him, I just felt fucked up.

"Son, did you really buy her a mini van," my mom called herself whispering.

"What else was he supposed to buy her, she got a whole football team of kids. He should have bought her a sprinter, scratch that, a fucking school bus." My sister was vicious as fuck and even if Jayda was the one for me, she would never make Amira's like list. Rumor was her best fucking friend, and she would cut me off before she did her.

"Excuse me, I wanted to thank you for visiting but would like to ask you to leave now so Remee and I can spend some time with the kids as a family." Jayda stood in front of us with a wide smile on her face. We all bust out laughing at the same time, this bitch was kinda funny.

RUMOR

*J*hated to admit it but staying with Rem, hasn't been
as bad as I thought it would be. I mean I felt like he
was fucking dragging it at this point, because it had been a few
weeks and Laya was fine. The doctors confirmed, but he
insisted we stay, and her traitorous ass agreed, only wanting to
leave and go to Miss Layla's and see her new puppy. It was
almost like the whole Jayda thing never happened. At first, I
thought that bitch was going to be around or at least her son,
but aside from her blowing up Remee's cell a few times, she was
like a fucking ghost. He hadn't brought the baby around even
though it was his, so I had no idea what was going on. Maybe he
felt like I would be mad if he brought him over, but honestly, I
wouldn't have been. None of this was his fault, and Remee was
his father. But in true Remee fashion, he wasn't about to
communicate. He was going to act like nothing even happened.

I can't say that I helped the situation that much. After the
first night I slept with him I had been back in his bed every
night, laid up like he was my nigga. It felt like I would never
learn. That was one of the reasons I made the decision to leave
this week.

"Two more days Laya, and we are going home. You been with daddy long enough." She stood in the doorway of her bedroom, arms crossed and a scowl on her face. It was in these moments she resembled the man who claimed to be her father but wasn't. She certainly had his bad attitude. I was almost for sure she would be my last one.

"Oh yea, two more days? When the fuck you was about to tell me? Or you was just going to try and sneak the fuck up outta here with my kid?"

"Remee, stop being so fucking dramatic oh my God. That's why she over there acting like she is auditioning for a part in a movie with that attitude. I have my own life, my own bed, and home. I want to get back to my shit. Laying around your crib all day and we not even friends isn't what I would call a good time. She can come back next week, without me."

"Oh that's on word? We not even friends?" He backed me into the wall and looked down at me. My body reacted even when my mind said stop. I swear my pussy was just a dirty bitch. I could feel how hard Remee was through his jeans, and I was wetter than the fucking ocean.

"Nigga move," I said shoving at his chest, but it didn't do anything, he was so much stronger than me. I was playing myself.

"Naw, I ain't moving no fucking were. I ain't ya friend Rumor? You not fucking wit ya nigga no more? I thought you understood that even when we not together, its always going to be you and me." His lips were damn near touching my ear as his deep voice flowed through my body. "That's why ya pussy acting out right now, she knows the fucking deal."

He stepped back, and I damn near ran into the room to start packing my shit. I wasn't the one who wanted to be done with us, he made that choice to basically dump me, so now he had to stand behind that decision. "Mommy, daddy said we are going shopping," A'Laya said dancing around the room. Her ass wasn't even old enough to know what shopping was, but she sure found ways to spend Remee's money.

"Who is we?" I asked praying it wasn't me and her. I was looking forward to a bubble bath, a glass of wine and relaxing.

"Sure, the fuck ain't me," Remee said with his lip curled. He hated the mall, crowds were not his thing. I shook my head, no. Laya was going to have to wait until another day. "Come on ma, don't be a meany. Cahir dropped her off a bag of sneakers earlier and she needs some clothes to match." Sighing I knew I was going to the mall. I made a mental note to curse Cahir out later. My child had enough clothes to cover a small orphanage.

"Fine, we ain't going in no damn Disney store either."

"Cool, I have to handle some business, go in the safe and grab some money." I nodded not really paying him any attention. I was too busy texting Amira so she could meet me at the mall. I hated shopping alone, and since it was on Remee, I planned to tear the mall the fuck up. She agreed to meet me at the house so we could ride together. I decided to get dressed before I did anything else. She didn't live far, so I knew she would be here soon.

I handled my hygiene and threw on some maroon tights, a blue cropped shirt with a maroon stripe and a pair of blue Balenciaga's. I decided to have A'Laya wear her blue Balencia-ga's too, except she had on a pair of white shorts and a blue Tommy shirt. "Mommy, auntie is here," her tiny voice yelled from the top of the stairs.

"Ok, let me grab some money and we can go." Going into the master closet I typed in the code and the back wall slid over. Then I entered the code to the safe. I grabbed a stack of money, and something fell out of the safe. I bent down to pick it up, but as soon as I saw what it was my heart stopped. Slowly I ran my hand over the velvet box, a bunch of shit was going through my mind. Was Remee going to propose to Jayda. I bet that was why he broke up with me. I put the money away and closed the safe, keeping the ring box clutched in my hand.

I sank down to the floor because my legs felt weak. I thought about not opening the box, I seriously felt like my heart couldn't take anymore. Like my fingers had a mind of their own, and I was staring at one of the prettiest rings I had ever seen. I knew the moment I saw it, that this ring wasn't for Jayda, it was for me. Was Remee about to propose to me? I felt his presence, and I looked up to see a tear leave his eye.

"I'm sorry Ru."

Why was he apologizing if he was going to propose to me, why the fuck was he crying? I pulled the ring from the box and saw our names engraved; it was definitely mine. Then it hit me like a fucked-up epiphany. He was going to marry me, until Jayda popped up pregnant.

BELLA

J sat back on the couch and watched as Sire paced back and forth in front of me. Shit didn't end well with Jax the other day at my job. All I could do was snatch my hand from Jax's and step back, praying they didn't cut up too bad and get me fired. Jax threw out some lame ass apology and tried to dap Sire up. Once he pulled out his gun and went upside that nigga's head a few times I realized shit was going left. I know it looked bad on my end, but it wasn't my fault his friend was a damn creep. And even though he had lied to me, I didn't want Sire to believe I was that type of bitch. But he still needed to go home. I just spent the last two weeks damn near a hostage in my own crib. All this nigga let me do was go to work and school then come home. He would be waiting for me inside the job every night and would even be posted up outside my classroom. I really was wondering how the fuck he got my schedule.

"Sire, this shit can't keep up. You have business to handle and a whole ass family. And as for me, I have a life I need to get back to. My real life, one that doesn't involve you. To be honest, I don't want to see your face, not every fucking day, not at all." It was hard to keep a straight face and tell that lie. I loved seeing Sire's face. I wouldn't give him any pussy, for obvious reasons, but just having him in my bed at night next to me and waking up to his tatted arms around me was life.

"So that's it shorty? It's just fuck me? You don't want me around at all? If I disappeared out this mother fucker right now you not bout to feel no way about the shit?" He was giving me a puppy dog look, his face looking extra sad and shit. Little did he know his sad face wasn't moving me.

"Come on Sire what did you think was about to happen? I was going to say fuck it you got someone but I'm still about to sleep wit you. If I was that kind of female, you wouldn't even want to be with me. I would only be some pussy to you. I deserve more than that. Even if it don't seem like I deserve better, I do. And if I were that down on myself, I would have just fucked wit ya homeboy. Shit at least he didn't have a family at home." His face went from sad to pissed in a matter of seconds. I guess me saying I would fuck with Jax struck a nerve. He walked over to where I was sitting on the couch fast as hell causing me to scoot back as far as I could.

Instead of snatching me up, he crouched down so that we were eye level. "Oh, you should have just fucked with Jax? That's ya motherfucking word?" I shrugged and looked to the left of him breaking our eye contact. "Why don't you understand that you mean something to me Bells? You got a nigga's heart." His phone went off a few times, and a look of frustration crossed his face. I knew it was her, he didn't even have to say it and as much as I told myself it didn't matter, it did. "Bella-"

"Nigga just go. The fuck you still standing here talking to me for and your bitch is calling. Run along." He reached out his hand to try and grab mine, but I snatched it away. I went from feeling broken-hearted to being pissed just that fast. "Sire leave!" I snapped. He stood there for a few minutes watching me, not saying shit before he walked out and left. I rolled over and cried into the couch pillows until I finally fell asleep.

* * *

I LOOKED IN THE FRIDGE A SECOND TIME WISHING SOME FOOD would magically appear. I didn't feel like going to the grocery store, but I knew Eternity would be dropping the kids off later and they had to eat. Slipping on a pair of black tights, a black t-shirt with a gold Nike logo on the front and a pair of black and gold Pink slides, I felt plain but comfortable. I grabbed a hair tie and pulled my hair up into a messy bun, that seemed like all I did to it these days. My energy was drained from all the sadness I had been feeling, and my hair was the least of my worries.

Walking outside to wait on my Uber, I half expected Sire to be hiding in the bushes waiting to take me where I had to go. But ever since I shouted at him to leave the other day I hadn't seen or heard from him. My brain said good, let that cheating ass nigga stay gone. But my heart was missing him. The Nissan Altima pulled up in front of me and I checked to make sure the license plate matched what my app had before getting in. I was too cute to be kidnapped. I kept my AirPods in the whole ride to the store, listening to a bunch of what I called in my feelings music. I smiled at the driver once we pulled up, rated him five stars and sent a small tip. I had a list written out in a pretty pink sparkly notebook.

I made it halfway through the store before I heard his voice. He sounded angry, that was new for Sire. He usually sounded calm. He was even funny sometimes. Whoever he was in the store with was pissing him off. It didn't take long before him and his girl came into view. She was pushing their cart that had a bunch of TV dinners, chips and other bullshit. They looked like couple goals, her rocking a Gucci dress and Gucci sandals. Her hair and make up was on point. She looked good next to the man I loved. I tried not to stare and gave myself a pep talk at the same damn time. *The dick wasn't even that good,* I lied. Giggling at my own dumb shit, I turned the corner and ran right into someone. *Shit.*

"Oh my God, I'm sorry," I squealed as I offered the sexy stranger a smile.

"No problem beautiful." A grin came across his face and I blushed. He wasn't necessarily my type, I liked taller men, and it didn't help that he was dressed in khakis and a polo. But shit maybe having a type was my problem. I needed to be looking for the exact opposite of what I had been messing with. "I'm Chris," he added, holding out his hand for me to shake.

"Hi, I'm Arabella," I replied. As I went to shake his hand, he moved fast to gently grab it and bring it to his lips. After lightly kissing the tops of my fingers, he let my hand go.

"Go check out, I will meet you at the car," I heard Sire snap behind me. I knew he was about to be on some shit and sure enough as soon as I turned around, he was headed my way, his face filled with a murderous look. He didn't seem to give a fuck that his girl was standing at the end of the aisle watching his every move. Apparently, she wasn't meeting him at the car.

"Hey, my nigga, she said sorry, now move the fuck on."

"I wasn't talking to you, and by the looks of it, you're here with your woman already. So, I think you should back off and mind your business," Chris said. He narrowed his eyes examining Sire like he could beat him.

Wham! Sire punched him so hard I swear I heard his jaw crunch. Chris damn near dropped to the ground. He was only saved by clinging on to the edge of the cart. I closed my eyes in embarrassment. I didn't know whether to apologize or just run away. Chris saved me from a decision when he turned and jogged towards the front of the store. "Really Sire, what the fuck is wrong with you?" I hissed in his direction. "You in here wit ya people and bothering me. You are not my MAN," I made sure to emphasize man, hoping he would get the fucking point.

"Come on Bells, you seriously about to hop on the next nigga's dick? For what to get over me, or try and make me mad?" He was glaring at me while talking his dumb shit.

"What the fuck you trying to say, that I'm a hoe or something? Urghh," I damn near yelled as I turned to go and finish my shopping. I was glad his people were nowhere to be found as I picked up my last few items and went to stand in line. As soon as I heard my total, I groaned inwardly. I overspent. Dealing with Sire and his bullshit put me off my game, and I was just grabbing shit.

"Your total is three hundred dollars and sixty-seven cents. Cash or credit?" The bubbly cashier was getting on my nerves. Like who the fuck is that happy about spending all this damn money.

"Credit," Sire said as he slid his card before I could stop him. "Thanks Jessica," he said smiling as she handed him my receipt. I decided not to even waste my breath advising him on how I didn't want him buying shit for me, now or moving forward.

"You don't say thank you?"

"Nigga, thanks for what? Beating up some poor man I ran into, calling me a hoe or paying for shit I could have paid for myself. Naw, fuck you." I tried to push my cart outside the door, but he stopped me.

"Come on, I'm taking you home." My face must have reflected my thoughts because he chuckled. "She drove herself shorty, I only came to give her some money for some toy my baby girl wanted. You should ask, not assume. I ain't even fucked her since you been back in my life. Shit with Shay just is what it is."

I followed him outside, not wanting to go with him but also

not in the mood to argue. "You not coming inside when we get there." I said as he loaded my groceries into the back of his Benz. I sat with my arms folded the whole ride to my place and lucky for him he didn't say a word.

"Yo I'm just going to carry your shit inside, I ain't trying to stay. So, don't fucking spazz on me or no dumb shit." Rolling my eyes, I took the bag with the eggs and left him to get everything else. It was petty, but I was about to stay on some petty shit. I was tired of being played. I sat on the couch and watched him carry in all the bags while I played in my phone. Once the last case of water was set on the counter, he turned to face me. "Come lock up," he said with an attitude. The fuck he mad for.

"Shorty, you know I wasn't calling you a hoe. I just don't want you wit no other nigga. Seeing him put his lips on ya skin had me fucked up." He stopped in the doorway, his tall body leaned against the frame.

"Sire, I can't be alone forever. You have someone, a life to live and a family to do it with. Me and Jael deserve the same thing. I can't be with you, so what else do you want me to do?" At this point I was curious to see what he thought was about to happen here. Like how the fuck you think we about to move forward from this shit.

"Bells, I just need you in my life. I know you not fucking wit me like that, but I will settle for your friendship. I'm not losing you again. You don't miss a nigga at all?" The way he was looking at me had me weak as fuck.

"Why did you lie? When you saw me in Burger King you could have told me you had someone. Let me make my own decisions on if I was fucking wit you or not. You made me into this grimy bitch, who just been fucking someone else's man. But that shit ain't fair because I didn't even know what was up."

"Shit at first I just didn't want to lose you, but then to be honest after awhile, I just forgot her ass existed. I was just happy as fuck to be spending time with you." I respected the fact that he was at least honest. He could have lied and told me some bullshit.

"Ok Sire, friends. But that doesn't mean you can beat up dudes who try and holla at me or be breaking in my house, tying me up or other crazy shit. I mean friends like you can call on the phone once in a while and say hey."

"Cool. So, you coming to our block party this weekend friend?"

"Uhhh, I think I will pass on that one," I said, my hand subconsciously going to my messy hair.

"Naw, I need you there. Go see my sister Friday and get your hair done. She been bothering my ass everyday about when you coming through. Just tell me what time and I will call and get you an appointment. And make sure you bring my princess. They got a ton of stuff for kids. She is going to have fun."

"Ok, I guess I could get it done Friday in the morning. And I'm only coming to the block party if I can bring Eternity and her son too."

"Yea, of course, bring whoever you want as long as it ain't no nigga. Now come kiss your friend because he got shit to do."

I laughed and tried to shove him out the door, but he held my arms and let his lips meet mine. I almost forgot our situation as his tongue slipped in my mouth. He broke the kiss and walked away with a smirk.

* * *

TODAY WAS THE DAY I WAS GETTING MY HAIR DONE AND I WAS nervous as fuck. Sire's sister seemed nice, but that was in front of him. Maybe she was going to fuck my shit up or come at me sideways. Females could be the worst, which was why I only had one damn friend. "I could have caught the bus," I lectured Sire as he knocked on my door. Well he wasn't using some stolen key, so that was baby steps.

"Naw, I keep telling you I don't want you out there like that. You know I can just get you your own shit. You got a license? Where my princess at?"

"Hell no, you can't buy me a car and yes I have a license. Jael is at daycare. I have to pay them for the full five days rather I work or not, so she went."

"You be doing her dirty as fuck. I thought she was getting her hair done too." He looked sad Jael wasn't home. Those two still made sure to hang out and she swore Sire was her best friend. The whole ride there I had butterflies in my stomach. I wasn't much of a people person. I was shy as fuck and liked blending into the background.

He pulled in front of the shop and looked over at me. "Why the fuck you look scared? My sister is the nicest out of the whole family. She likes you, trust me. If she didn't, we would all know. My sister in law is in there too, they not about to be on no bullshit, I promise." Taking a deep breath, I grabbed my Coach bag that had seen better days and slowly climbed out of the truck. I hoped this style didn't cost a lot. I wouldn't dare allow Amira to give me a free hairdo. But my money was tight, at least I had some extra from Sire buying my groceries the other day.

I walked inside and I felt like all eyes were on me. The conversation the women were having stopped and everyone was staring. "I'm looking for Amira, I have a ten o'clock appointment," I said, explaining my presence.

"Hey, Bella right? Your so pretty, Sire did not do you justice when he told me about you. Although I should have known, he hasn't stopped talking about you. Anyway, come sit down, Mira is coming out in a second. She ran to the back to get some more gel or something." Rumor came and hugged me before waving me to a chair. I was flattered that someone as beautiful as her was calling me pretty.

"Edge control, Ru, not gel. Hey future sister in law, sorry I kept you waiting. That's Rumor, my sister in law and my best friend, and over there is Sasha my head stylist and my other stylist's Patricia and Carmen." She snapped a pretty purple cape with a silver and black logo on the front before snapping it around my neck.

"You know I'm not dating your brother," I said trying to set the record straight as she began shampooing me. "We are just friends. He is happy with his girl and I'm happy being single." She looked at Rumor and the two of them burst out laughing.

Girl keep telling yourself you're his friend. My brother has never been the way he is about you with any female. Hell, the way he talks about you, I bet you could ask for some shit I couldn't even get. I mean don't use my brother, but make sure you get some shit you want." I shook my head at her laughing. The morning went by fast, me, her and Rumor chatted away, and I really liked them. Rumor didn't seem to be getting her hair done so I felt like she had just come to be nosey and see me. I couldn't lie and say I wouldn't do the same.

"Ok, you are done. I hope you like it, since you really didn't tell me what you wanted, and my talking ass never asked." She spun me around and I gasped. My normally wavy hair was bone straight, parted in the middle and flowing down my back. I ran my hand through the silky texture and let it drop back into perfect formation.

"I love it, thank you so much. I usually just wash my hair and throw some moose in it, then pray my curls don't get too frizzy." I looked in the mirror one more time before grabbing my purse. "How much do I owe you?" I asked.

"The fuck you doing Bella," Sire said appearing out of nowhere. I must have been so busy looking at myself I didn't hear him come in. "You trying to make me look like a sucka ass nigga." He handed his sister a few hundred-dollar bills before he came to stand near me. He pulled me in his arms and ran his hands through my hair. "Damn babe, you look fine as fuck," he whispered before burying his face in my neck and kissing my neck. My body reacted, my nipples were hard, and my pussy was aching to feel him. By the way he palmed my ass, he knew what was up. And, I knew this friend shit was going to be a problem.

SIRE

I looked at Shay and shook my head. She had on the tightest one-piece short shit she could find. Her whole pussy print was on display, her fresh thirty inches of weave were flowing down her back in black waves and her acrylic nails were an eye-catching neon pink. I was amused and pissed at the same time and for more than one reason. First of all, my daughter stood next to her, hair in two crooked barely done ponytails. Her clothes thank God were fresh as hell, a peach and white colored Polo dress and matching flip flops. The second part of the not so funny fucking joke was that I knew Shay thought she was about to roll wit me to the block party. Yea this shit was funny.

"Aight be good, we out," I said as I grabbed Tayari in my arms and she waved like she didn't give a fuck she was leaving her mom.

"Ummm I'm ready too so what the fuck you mean you out? Nigga I know you're kidding if you think you're leaving without me." She was pointing her finger in my face, ready to get that mah fucka broke.

I stroked my chin and gave her a look, so she knew to calm

80

down. God knows I ain't want to put hands on a female; I wasn't that kind of nigga. But she was about to take me there. She always took me there. "Naw, you not rolling with us. Matter of fact you not going at all. Sit ya hot ass in the house, clean up or something. Do some good girlfriend shit. The fuck you want to go to a family event dressed like that for. Looks like you out here trying to catch a new nigga or summin." If she only knew I welcomed that outcome.

"Oh, so I can't go to a party open to the public? Nigga you got me fucked up! I promise I will be there. Watch me. You think you about to have my daughter over there wit ya other bitch. I ain't fucking stupid." I wanted to check her on calling Bella a bitch, but then I would be admitting to fucking with someone else.

"Watch ya mouth in front of her." I barked as I turned my daughter in my arms, so she was facing the door instead of her crazy ass mother. "I said what I said." I wasn't about to argue wit Shay's ass today.

"What's so fucking special about her? Do you love her?" She said, standing in my face, crocodile tears forming in the corners of her eyes.

"Yo on some real shit, stop asking questions you can't handle the answer to."

"I know it was that ugly ass girl from Target the other day," she said, causing me to stop at the doorway. Shaking my head, I walked out of the house leaving Shay standing there to believe whatever the hell she wanted,

It was still early, but I prayed Amira hadn't left the shop yet. I hit her number as I buckled my daughter in the back of my royal blue Maserati. "What Sire, I'm busy as hell."

"Well damn, hello to you too. I need you to do something to Tayari's hair. I can't bring her anywhere looking like this." I glanced in the rearview mirror, angry that her mother didn't take more pride in how our shorty looked.

"Sorry, you know I would do anything for my Tay Tay, but I really can't. I have two clients I have to finish before I can go and get ready for the party. Remee already warned me about coming too late, and he needs my help to set up. Maybe you could try Rumor?"

Shit. I knew Rumor was busy managing the vendors for today. "Aight sis no problem. I will figure something out." I drove to Bella's house, hoping she wouldn't be on no wild shit. Lately, she was so busy fighting her feelings for me that I never knew how she was going to be feeling. I decided to ring the bell today instead of letting myself in. I gave her a copy of the key I had, but believe me I had more. I would never let the girl I loved, and her shorty live somewhere I couldn't access. The world was filled with crazy mahfuckas, and I needed to know they were good at all times. Thinking about the way Cahir told me he broke into her home girl's spot, I felt like I had proven my point.

"Sire, everything ok?" Bella asked, slowly opening the door. "Hi there, aren't you the prettiest little girl," she said, causing Tayari to smile shyly, then hide her face.

"Hey, I didn't mean to just pop up, but Amira is booked solid, and my daughter needs her hair fixed for today. Nothing fancy, maybe just a fresh ponytail or something. I umm didn't really know who else to call." She looked at me funny and was probably thinking what about her mother, but Bella was too sweet to say that shit in front of my baby.

"No problem, come in and give me a minute to get a comb and stuff." She smiled again, more for Tayari's benefit than mine I was sure.

"Sire," Jael shouted as she ran up to me and hugged my legs. "Are you coming to the fair with us?" I looked at Bella, confused as hell.

"She keeps calling the block party a fair since I said they had a bounce house." She laughed, and so did I. Kids always come up with funny shit.

"You and mommy are coming with me," I said lightly pinching her cheek. She focused her attention to my daughter, who was just watching with wide eyes. "Hi, you want to play," Jael said.

"This is Tayari, Tay this is Jael and her mommy Bella. Can you say hi?"

"Hi," she said before she flung her arms around my neck and hid again. She really needed to spend more time with other kids aside from A'Laya. "She can play after she gets her hair done." I moved further inside and set my baby on the couch. I set the Gucci book bag I carried with her stuff in it on the table and sunk down next to her.

"Is she going to cry?" Bella asked as she gently removed the ponytail holders from her hair.

"Naw, Amira been braiding and combing her hair since she was a baby."

"Ummm Sire, I have to wash her hair, I wouldn't feel right doing her hair and its this dirty. Does she have something else to slip on, so her clothes don't get wet.

I was mad as fuck that her mom really didn't give a fuck about my shorty. "I have extra clothes for her in her bag, let me see if there is something."

"No, it's cool, I have some of Jael's old pajamas that she outgrew, they are clean. She can throw them on." She grabbed my daughter and carried her upstairs, the whole time holding some type of conversation with her. Whatever she was saying had my shorty laughing.

I must have fallen asleep because soon enough, I heard tiny laughs. Opening my eyes, I saw Tayari and Jael playing with dolls on the floor. Jael's hair was on point, she had a few braids in the front that ended in white barrettes, and the rest of her hair was in two cute ponytails, with those little ball things in white and gold, holding them together. The whole scene had me smiling hard as hell. In a perfect world this would be my life. "Good your up, I'm making them a quick lunch and we can leave. Is there anything she cannot eat? I was just going to give them peanut butter and jelly sandwiches, milk and apple sauce."

"She cannot have cows' milk, only soy or almond milk. Thanks for asking." She tilted her head to the side and looked at me oddly.

"Oh, ok no problem. They can have some Juicy Juice. But there was milk in her sippy cup, just so you know. I dumped it and washed it since I didn't know how fresh it was." I could tell she was uncomfortable telling me, but this shit wasn't her fault. I had to just start keeping my daughter with me more because clearly, I can't depend on Shay to care for her properly.

"Aight, I appreciate you ma." I watched as she fed the kids, cleaned them up and dressed them both in their nice clothes. Jael was matching Tayari's fly with a cute Polo jean dress and some pink Polo slip-on sneakers. Bella was sexy as always. I don't even think she tried hard. She was just one of those naturally pretty chicks. I was annoyed she wouldn't let me buy her an outfit for today, she should have been rocking some high-end shit right along wit me. Shorty was dressed casually, rocking a grey t-shirt dress with a picture of Marylin Monroe holding a pink lollipop. On her feet, she was rocking a pair of white, pink and grey Air Max. Her hair was still straight, and she left it loose, so it was hanging down her back.

I smiled when she picked up the cream and grey Louie bag that I copped her. When I gave it to her last night, she tried to give it back, but I left that shit anyway. "Damn you done eye-fucking me," she said low enough, so the kids didn't hear.

"Hell naw, I ain't never done with that. You ready?"

"Yep, I put some little biker shorts under Tayari's dress since they are going to be running around and stuff."

She grabbed up the book bag that I noticed she had put

snacks and juices in, and both girls' hands like Tayari was her kid too. "You so fucking perfect," I said following behind her. "Wife material."

"Yep, I just need to find a husband," she shot at me.

I glared at her as she got the kids in the car. "Don't get fucked up Arabella." She smirked and closed the car door, leaving me standing there.

I pulled up to Genesee street and pulled in the park. Over the years, we changed up how we did this shit. One of the main things was the amount of security we had. I pulled past the orange cones and parked next to Cahir's Lamborghini. I picked up Tayari, but she pulled away from me and reached for Bella. "Oh, you a traitor huh, it's cool, remember that next time you want some cookies or some shit." I handed my baby over, and I swear she stuck her tongue out at me.

"It's ok Sire, I will hold your hand," Jael said, looking up at me with a grin like she knew how I felt. I grabbed her hand in mine, and we walked over to the tables reserved for the family.

"Sup lil nigga took you long enough," Remee said as I dapped him and Cahir up. He was always talking shit. But he his attitude had been worse lately. Not being with Rumor turned him cold. He only smiled for A'Laya.

"I see you on ya family shit, she's a good look for you," Cahir said, looking towards Bella as she hugged Amira and Rumor. "And the girls like her, you better not fuck this up." Shit I wasn't trying to come out here on no family shit, but I wasn't mad about it. I hadn't even intended to bring Tayari around Bella. It felt right and foul as fuck at the same time.

"Yo shorty, you good," I said, walking up behind her as she helped Tayari fix her shoe.

"Yea, just waiting on Eternity to get here. She better show up," she said, side-eyeing my cousin. Yea I could see her girl wanting to avoid his ass, he had some screws loose.

"Well well well ain't this some cute happy family type shit. I wonder if my girl knows you out here playing house with... Shit who the fuck are you?" Jayda's ghetto behind asked, staring Bella up and down.

"She ain't none of your fucking business, so move around bitch," Rumor said, stepping in front of Bella. I could see the anger rolling off of her in waves and even though I knew she liked Bella, I could tell this shit was personal. Remee stood there watching, waiting to fuck Jayda up if she got close to Rumor. He never asked Jayda where their son was, shit I had never even seen him with the little boy. I needed to make sure my brother was good sooner than later because this shit wasn't like him.

"Raggedy side bitch, I wasn't asking you." Jayda took a few steps closer, and so did her hoe ass cousin Lolo. Laya ran to her mothers' side most likely about to come to her mother's rescue, and I knew at that moment that shit was about to go left.

"Amira, take the kids to go play. Now." She snatched all three girls up fast as hell and got them out of there. I nodded to one of the security guards to follow.

Rumor pulled her long braids up in a ponytail holder, causing the sun to shine on her diamond Rolex. I wondered if Jayda really thought she was a side chick. There wasn't shit Ru wanted that my brother didn't buy her. She didn't even have to ask, just look. "I got ya bitch right here." Rumor bust Jayda in the mouth damn near dropping her. She didn't even stop just kept swinging until Lolo grabbed her hair.

Before any of us could intervene, Bella chopped Lolo in the throat, causing her to choke, stumble and fall into the grass. She kicked her a few times and stomped her in the back of the head. "Snake ass bitch, if they want to fight let them fight fair," she hissed as she fucked shorty up. Finally, Cahir had security drag them out of our area. I hope he ran those bitches home.

"Foul ass nigga, you letting her fight your baby mama and shit. You know I just had your son Remee, he needs me. And fuck you too Sire, I'm calling Shay right now so she can come and get her daughter." She was yelling so loud, half the people there were looking our way. I chuckled because we both knew the last thing Shay was doing was coming to get Tayari. She never wanted to be bothered with our kid. I had to ask myself again why I didn't just leave her. I guess I planned on it when the timing was right.

"Damn sis you a scrapper," Rumor commented as she hugged Bella. "Let's go find the kids, Laya is a fucking brat and can be a handful."

"Sire, I'm about to go and hang out with the kids. I hope me being here didn't cause any problems with your girlfriend." Bella had touched my hand and gave me a look of sadness.

"Man fuck that bitch. If he would just kill her like I advised him too this shit wouldn't be an issue." Cahir took a drink from his bottle of Patron like he didn't just say some off the wall shit. Bella was looking from me to him, trying to figure out if he was for real or not.

"Girl, he is dead ass serious, but just ignore him. Let's go," Rumor told her while shaking her head.

She still stood there waiting on me to say something, like I was her nigga. "Here hold this," I said, handing her a small knot of cash. She hesitated, and everyone laughed when Rumor snatched it and threw it in her purse. I pulled her in and kissed her before my people dragged her away.

"Shit your cheap ass giving a female some money, it must be love," Grip commented.

"Fuck you," I shot back as I grabbed my cell. Seeing Shay's name, I wasn't even surprised. "What," I barked into the phone as I walked off some for privacy.

"You got me fucked up. You out here with my daughter and your hoe. She better be gone when I get there." She was snapping and I just waited for her to take a breath.

"Shay leave me the fuck alone," I said hanging up right after.

ETERNITY

*M*y finger hovered over the reject button when Bella's name popped up for the third time in a row. I was doing all I could to avoid going to this block party mainly because I knew he would be there. Most likely with a bunch of bitches all over him. I didn't know what would bother me more, just being around him or seeing him with other women. "What Bella?"

"Bestie," she said, drawing out the word. "You promised you would come today. Are you ready!"

"You know I don't want to face him. This shit is unfair. Plus, you out there wit ya man, the fuck you need me around for?" I hoped she heard the pleading in my voice. For whatever reason, the thought of going to hang out with the McKenzie's had my anxiety on a thousand.

Girl, I came as a friend, he ain't my man. His girl's people done came over here, causing a fight. I got a lot to catch you up on. That's why I need you. I don't want to just be standing up here all day alone, random hoes coming for me. I owe you bestie!! Plus, Cass will have so much fun. There are games, candy, bounce houses. You name it. If you don't want to come for me, do it for my nephew." Sighing I thought about what she was saying. It did sound like fun for my son, and I wouldn't want to deny him over a nigga. Plus, if my bestie had beef I was there, no one was going to try no slick shit with my girl.

"Fine. I will get ready and be there soon. Don't whine either because it just started thirty minutes ago. Now bye." I hung up before she could say anything else. I threw myself back on the bed, thoughts of Cahir running through my mind. Maybe he won't come through until later on. Niggas like him looked like they couldn't be outside in the daylight. His evil ass might melt or some shit. I glared at my closet like it did some shit to me personally before finally getting up. I had a small shopping habit, so I knew I could find something to wear. I showered, brushed my teeth, then moisturized my skin. I slipped on the off the shoulder one-piece short romper I just bought. That shit hugged all my curves just right. It was a rose-pink color, and I had a pair of sandals from Aldo that matched perfectly. My hair was in some goddess braids, so I didn't have to do anything there. I was sure to put on some makeup before putting on my gold and diamond hoops and matching bracelet.

I didn't want to go true, but if I was going to show up, I was damn sure about to look fly. "Come on Cass, you ready?" He ran in the room looking like a little ass man. His jean shorts and black and yellow Jordan shirt matched his new 12's. I just had to spray him with cologne, throw his chain on and put some oil in his curls. "You so cute," I cooed as I kissed his face.

"Maaaa," he whined as we headed to my car. He wiped my kiss off, and I couldn't believe my baby was growing up on me. Being a mom was my greatest joy, and if the situation were better, I would have more kids. But with my pick in men, I had a better chance of waiting till I got my money up and adopting.

It took me longer to find parking than the drive to the park. This shit was packed, and I told myself if I didn't find a spot in three more minutes I was gone. I knew I could have called Bella and told her I needed parking, but I barely wanted to be here. "Mommy look a bounce house," Cassian called out excitedly pointing to the colorful inflated objects. Sighing, I flashed my baby a smile and kept circling the block. Finally, I saw someone about to pull out, and I swooped in and parked. I was glad I didn't wear heels because we had to walk what seemed hella far. "Yo ma," some dude called out to me, causing me to move a little faster. The whole way to the roped-off area niggas kept calling out to me, saying crazy shit about my fat ass. Just straight disrespectful since they see I was out here wit my son.

I stopped in front of the two big ass dudes they had standing by the entrance. "Hey, I'm meeting my homegirl Bella over here," I explained, waiting to be let past.

"Naw baby girl this a private area, so you gonna have to meet up wit ya people somewhere else." I was annoyed, pulling out my cell phone. I dialed Arabella, but the phone rang out. It was loud as fuck over here with all the music, so she probably couldn't hear shit. I made a face and turned around with a huff. I was about to go home. I should have stayed my ass in the house watching TV.

"Damn cutie, my bad, you can meet up wit me later if your friend fronted on you," the second guard called out. I turned and gave him the nastiest look I could.

"She good," Ransom said, stepping up to the toy cops. Funny now how he was always Ransom to me these days. I felt like Cahir was someone who cared about me; that person was dead now. His face was emotionless like normal, and I felt a chill. I walked past him, gripping Cassian's hand. "Sup lil man," he greeted my son, causing him to stop dead in his tracks to dap him up. "Your girl over there," he said, looking towards a table near the grill."

"Thanks," I responded, wishing he would say something else. Instead, he started doing something on his phone. "Well fuck you," I muttered as Bella, Jael and two other girls made their way over to me.

"Fuck you too," Ransom snapped back as he wandered away.

"Bestie you made it," Bella said as she ran over to hug me. "You look so cute. I bet that's why he has an attitude."

"Girl he ain't thinking about me, and I'm sure as fuck not thinking about him." She gave me a yeah right look but didn't say anything else on the topic.

"Rumor, Amira, this is my best friend Eternity and her son Cassian. Eternity these are Sire's sisters Amira and Rumor. And his daughter Tayari," she said, pointing to the little girl she held securely in her arms. My eyes bucked and I couldn't wait to get the tea on how the fuck she ended up playing house at the biggest outdoor event of the summer with Sire's kid. After the girls gave me hugs, we made our way to the table where everyone else was. I noticed that Rumor and Amira kept giving me strange looks and I almost wondered had I did something wrong or was my titty hanging out.

"They just trying to figure out how Ransom knows you," Sire said smirking. I guess they heard him and me talking. Great. I just shook my head hoping Ransom would stay wherever the fuck he was at for the rest of the day.

"Come on, let's take the kids to the bouncy house," Rumor suggested. We got up to walk down the hill towards the crowds. I noticed that her and Remee didn't say shit to each other, but he made sure some nigga followed behind her and his daughter. I heard the rumors about their breakup. The club was filled with gossip. Personally, I wished they'd get back together. They seemed like they really loved each other. I made sure I took my drink with me, I needed something to take the edge off, and this Long Island was hittin'.

Two hours later, and these kids still weren't tired. My poor baby was the only little boy in our group, but he didn't seem to care. He and A'Laya were closer in age, and they got on the rides together. If I didn't know better, I would have thought my baby was crushing on her. "Umm do you guys know where the bathroom is. These drinks got me about to piss on myself."

"Over there, behind the spades tables. That's the building with the bathrooms." Amira pointed to the spot where a million niggas was crowding the tables.

"Ok, I will be right back, can you guys keep an eye on Cass." All the ladies said yes and I damn near ran to the bathroom. I peed, washed my hands and headed out feeling good, at least until I saw him standing in the cut. Ransom was leaned against a tree, some girl in his face. He was drinking something, not paying her any attention, at least until he saw me. Once he noticed me standing there, he tapped her on her shoulder and let his gaze lower. She immediately dropped to her knees and started to unbuckle his pants.

I felt like someone had punched me dead in the throat. I was for real struggling to breathe and my heart was pounding. He looked me dead in my eyes the whole time he fucked her face. It was like he took pleasure from two things, seeing my pain and causing her pain. The harder he slammed into her mouth, the more his eyes glazed with lust. The girl was trying to back up, but he held her tight by her long weave. Finally, he pulled out and sprayed his nut all over her face.

I ran back inside the bathroom, trying not to cry. As soon as I got in the stall I threw up. I hated this nigga.

CAHIR

$\mathcal{I}$ felt like shit for what I did to Eternity, but fuck it, that was the kind of nigga I was. Better she knows now; it will help her kill those fantasies that she had that I was someone nice. The look on her face while she watched me fuck Brandy's face was hard to watch. I wanted to throw the bitch to the ground and comfort Tee, but I also wanted to make her mad. And I knew that would do it. I was surprised she didn't leave, but I respected the fact she was making sure her little man had fun. I was openly stalking her at this point. It wasn't no fucking reason for me to be over here near the games and shit. And I wasn't hiding the fact I had my eye on her.

"So, you want to tell me about you and her," Rumor said as she came to stand next to me. I glared at her, hoping she would drop it. But of course, she wasn't, Rumor was like a fucking pitbull when she wanted to know something. "You like her, I can tell. I can also tell you fucked it up."

"I don't even fucking know that girl," I lied as I still watched Eternity. Cassian was playing some basketball game for little kids. He was good for his age. For some reason I had the urge to go over there and play with him. It was like this fucking girl had put a spell on me. I wasn't myself around her at all.

"I can just ask Remee," Rumor said, bringing my attention back to her. She was hopping from foot to foot and smiling. I swear we all spoiled her ass to the point she didn't understsand no.

"Come on Ru, you think that nigga on some hoe shit, about to sit up and gossip wit ya ass. Especially about me?" She pouted for a few minutes, knowing what I said was right. My cousin wasn't built like that. Plus, he knew I fucked with Rumor, so if she needed to know something I would have told her.

"Well I like her, and I hope you can fix whatever it is you did. I am not giving up on true love. If it ain't for me, it has to be for somebody. And Cahir, you deserve it." Her eyes got sad, and I knew she was thinking about my fucked-up childhood.

"Don't do that Ru, I'm good, all that did was make me stronger." *And dead inside* I thought to myself. "Stop fucking saying love ain't for you. That nigga Remee loves ya dirty draw-ers. You could stab that nigga in the heart, and he would still love you. Rem just handled shit the way niggas do, without thinking shit through. But you know you the one for him. You out here believing all the shit that cum bucket Jayda saying. I could see it today when she was talking shit. You didn't even have to fight that bitch. What the fuck you proving? You got what she wants." She started to shake her head, and I stopped her.

"Yes, you do. The funny thing is even though you got Remee's heart, that's not what Jayda desires. She wants the shit you don't give a fuck about. His money, his time, his loyalty. She will never have that. Ma, you got on a fifty thousand-dollar watch, and I don't even want to know how much the rest of that shit cost. You got a bad ass truck and be honest the only reason you don't have more cars is because you drive all his shit. You can live anywhere, travel anywhere. And most of all, you and

Laya are secure. He made sure of it. If my cousin ain't around and me and Sire ain't around y'all still good. That nigga put you first in a lot of ways. That's what she wants, a meal ticket. To be able to tell the hood she fucked a McKenzie."

She hugged me, "Cahir, you know you my favorite right."

"Hell, yea I know." My response caused her to giggle. She didn't move, and I knew she still wanted to get info on Eternity and me. She was going to be waiting for a long ass time. I didn't want anyone in my business.

Cassian made a shot and jumped up and down in celebration. That shit caused him to move back into the crowd and right on some dude's feet. "I'm sorry," Eternity said, helping Cass to his feet and speaking to the nigga. "Cassian, say sorry baby," she coaxed. My lil nigga looked like he was about to cry as the stranger looked at him with a scowl on his face. That shit had me tensing up. He better tighten the fuck up, he acted like a grown man stepped on his shit.

"I'm sorry," Cass said, his voice sounded tougher than he looked.

"Fuck your sorry lil mahfucka. Somebody is buying me some new sneakers out this bitch, unless you want to give me some pussy to make it up to me." He licked his dry ass lips as he looked Eternity up and down.

"He said sorry, he is a child, this is a children's area. Accidents happen. I'm sure the dirt will wipe right off." I could hear the irritation in Eternity's voice.

"Lil bad ass, you gone pay for my shit," this cornball said as he tried to reach for Cassian. I swear I felt Rumor smirk from behind me as I damn near ran over there. I snatched Cassian in my arms and looked at this pussy.

"Nigga you threatening my shorty over some dusty ass shoes?" He couldn't even speak, the fear in his eyes told me he already knew who I was. In case he forgot I pulled up my shirt showing him my heat.

"Yo I'm sorry Ransom, I didn't know. My bad."

"You saying sorry to the wrong fucking people." I was mad he asked Eternity for some pussy, but I was more pissed at how he talked to her son. I wanted to break his neck and send his body to his momma for her to see the bitch she raised got what he needed.

"I'm sorry lil man, and you too shorty. I really ain't mean none of that." He looked at me again before taking off into the crowd. I could see by the look on Tee's face she was ready to go. By now, Bella and Rumor were standing next to her, making sure she was good.

"Tee you aight?" I asked.

She could barely look at me, and I knew that was because of the shit earlier. "Yea I'm ok. Come on, Cassian we are about to leave." Just the look on his face let me know he was about to be on some hell no type of shit. But instead of crying or throwing a tantrum, he turned to me.

"Thank you, Cahir. I have to go now."

"He good, me and him about to go hang out. He don't need to be chilling with all these females anyway."

"Umm, I don't think that's the best idea." She said, reaching for her son. I almost said fuck it, but for some reason, I wanted to spend time with him. Take him to watch the basketball tournament, maybe put him on some rides or some shit.

"Come on Tee, why everything wit you got to be a fight. Ask Rumor; I'm actually good with kids. I just don't be around a lot of them. But I spend time with my little cousin every week."

"Girl A'Laya has him wrapped around her little fingers. I mean yeah Remee spoils her, but Uncle Cahir be doing big shit. That's why her little ass walking around with a Gucci purse and a children's Rolex. Her father and I wasn't approving any of that shit. She even painted Cahir's nails once." Rumor went on to tell all my fucking business causing me to mug her before she got too far with this shit.

"Ok, I guess for a little while. If he needs me, please call me. I have my cell right here." She said, holding up the phone in her hand. She still looked skeptical as fuck as we walked off.

"Aight Cass, what you want to go do," I asked as we walked away.

"Basketball," he said. I headed over to the courts to watch the games. I had some money on a few of the teams out here. Not because I needed it, I just bet for fun. I would always give the teams half if I won, most of these dudes were still in high school struggling. I saw more than a few people eyeing me curiosity all over their faces. I was sure I would be the talk of the block party. Bitches and niggas alike wondering if I had a kid and who the mama was. None of that shit really bothered me though. I was a man who did what I wanted and fuck the rest of the world.

I took a seat on the bottom bleacher closest to the court. "Yo move over some," I barked at some bitch I smashed a while back. Her hoe ass kept sliding down, trying to get closer to me. "I don't want you breathing on him." Cassian laughed then tried to scowl at her just like I did. He was a good kid, shit when I was with Laya, she was talking my ears off about everything. But Cassian just set next to me, his elbow propped up on my leg, his head in his hand. He was fascinated by the game, and I could tell basketball was going to be his thing. I wondered if his pops took him to games or some shit. I never thought to ask Eternity about her baby father, but now I was curious.

"You like basketball Cass."

"Yep." He responded, nodding his tiny head.

"Your dad be watching basketball with you?" Suddenly he sat straight up, his eyes wide with fear. I knew that kind of fear. I lived it as a kid. His tiny body was stiff, and he had even clenched his fists.

"No, my daddy is a bad man. He hurts my mommy. Do you know my daddy?"

I wanted to ask him what the fuck he meant by he hurts his mommy, but I knew he was too young to provide details. "Naw I don't know that nigga. But don't worry he ain't gonna hurt your mama again. I got ya'll." He relaxed and leaned his small body into mine. A few minutes later, he was watching the game again. Man hearing his pops was putting his hands on Eternity had me feeling some kind of way and whether she wanted to or not we were going to discuss this shit later on.

I kept Cassian wit me the rest of the day. I let him get on some rides and all that other shit. I swear his mom called me about a hundred times, making sure he was good. But at least she gave a fuck about her kid. I knew a lot of bitches that didn't. "You ready to go find your mom," I asked since it was getting dark.

"Ok," Cass said, following me. As soon as he saw his mom, he ran up to her and started talking. "I had so much fun. I watched basketball and went on rides and had cotton candy and ice cream." She was frowning at me when he told her all the junk food I let him eat.

"Give ya mom your money," I said. He reached in his pocket and handed her the cash he won when he helped me play craps.

"Where the hell he get money from Ransom?"

"I shot the dice mommy," he said ratting me out.

"Damn homie that was supposed to be a secret. You broke the code." I laughed so he knew he wasn't in trouble. Shit from the look on Eternity's face I was.

"Cassian go sit with auntie Bella and watch the fireworks. Say bye." He waved and ran off to do as he was told. "Ransom, look, I appreciate you helping out with that dude today, and it was sweet of you to spend time with my son. But you don't fuck wit me, and you made it clear from the jump you not a fan of kids and I don't want him confused. So, let's not do this again." She tried to walk away, but I grabbed her arm.

"Since when you call me Ransom?" That shit bothered the fuck out of me for some reason.

"Since you told me my pussy was trash. I'm about to leave, so take care of yourself, Ransom." She made sure to emphasize my street name before snatching out of my grasp and going to get her son. "Come on Cassian, we parked far, and it's dark, I don't want to be walking around all late."

"Give me your keys, and I will take you home. Eternity don't say shit to piss me off, you not about to be out here with all these wild hood mah fuckers walking around and shit." Her homegirl laughed, but she rolled her eyes. I see she still reached in her purse and got the damn keys. I grabbed them and motioned for this nigga Lo. "Go grab her car and drop it at the address I'm about to text you."

"Aight, where you parked ma?"

"I'm on Congress, a silver Camry." Lo nodded and took off. I couldn't believe she parked so fucking far.

"The fuck you park all the way over there for? We had spots closer for the family. You should have called your girl."

"I ain't family first of all, and I have legs I can walk. I didn't plan on staying this long. Shit, I didn't even want to come."

"Because of me?"

"Yea," she confirmed, making me sad. I was already regretting giving her a ride home. Any time I was around Eternity, I started to feel shit. I wasn't interested in being anything but what I was most of the time, numb.

REMEE

I sat back on the bed, looking at the Hennessey bottle on my nightstand. Lately, that was the only thing that had been keeping me company. Since Rumor found that ring, she didn't fuck with me period. We were in the same space the whole day of the block party, and she didn't say a word to me. She would drop off A'Laya or pick her up, all in silence, her face blank. I missed her. I asked myself a million times a day how the fuck I thought I was going to give her up. Now that she was gone, I had never felt so low.

I looked at my phone, scrolling the pictures I had of Rumor. The last one was of her and me. She had me taking some goofy ass selfie the day we had took Laya to see Disney on Ice. Going to wifey in my phone I clicked the name. It rang so many times I didn't think she was going to pick up. "Yes, Remee, what do you want?" She said as she picked up. Her voice was filled with annoyance, and it had me feeling like shit.

"Come through the house and chill wit me." She sucked in air like I had hit her.

"Rem, you must be smoking that shit. I sure the fuck ain't coming to your house, or anywhere wit you." She said that shit like something was wrong wit a nigga. Hearing the hate in her voice hit different.

"You hate a nigga for real huh."

"Yes, I do." She didn't even hesitate when she said that shit, and that was the worst part.

"Bring A'Laya over here and let me holla at you for a minute."

"I will bring her to your moms. Get her from there." She hung up in my face. I picked up the Hennessey bottle and threw it at the wall. I watched the dark brown liquid drip down my grey wall and onto the broken glass. That shit felt like it represented my life right now.

* * *

"HELLO," I SLURRED INTO THE PHONE. I WAS DRUNK AND HIGH, I didn't have Laya for a few days, so I went to the club last night and got twisted. That shit was the only thing getting me through.

"Remee, you haven't come to see your son in a month. I know you didn't want this baby, but he is here. So, the least you could do is see him once in a while, act like you give a fuck." Hearing Jayda on the other end of the phone gave me an instant headache.

"You got ya check this month, right?"

"Yes, but-"

"But fucking nothing. That lil nigga being taken care of, so clearly, I give a fuck. You still breathing, I let him have a mother, so clearly, I'm doing what I need to. I will come through and grab him soon, my family wants to see him, now get off my line." I clicked end and rolled back over to go to sleep.

I woke up the next day still feeling fuzzy. I knew I overdid it. I was only getting up because one of my spots got robbed, and that meant we needed to have a meeting. I got up and hopped in the shower, brushed my teeth and got myself together. It was hot as fuck outside, so I just put on a beater, Armani boxers and a pair of red Armani cargo shorts. I pulled up to Remi` and parked next to my spot, as always Cahir was parked in mine. I wished he would open a fucking club and stay out of my shit. It wasn't bad before but ever since he let shorty get in his head, he damn near be in my spot more than I do.

Walking in my office, I kicked the chair he was sitting in, causing him to mean mug my ass. "Stay the fuck out my parking spot bitch ass nigga. You don't own this shit." I looked at his bloodshot eyes and wondered when he slept last. "You ever leave this mother fucker or you living here now?" I knew he wasn't going to answer.

"Put that nigga on salary, make him earn his keep since he wants to chill in this bitch twenty-four seven." Sire laughed at himself; I guess he thought he was funny. I sat down and checked my phones—no calls from Ru, but no surprise. The last time I spoke to her a few weeks ago was the last time and I was starting to get pissed.

"Fuck you lil nigga, we having this meeting because of some shit you got us in the middle of." That caused me to stop texting Rumor and pay attention. "Oh, I guess you didn't tell your brother how you got beef with one of our workers behind some pussy. Now the spot he runs was robbed and his ass is missing He shouldn't have been in charge of any fucking thing after you pistol-whipped his ass. He should have been fired, or better yet killed. You too fucking soft Sire, and you know what I ain't cleaning up your fucking mess. All I know is once you murk this nigga, all the money better be accounted for." Cahir said what he said, got up and left. Him and Sire where always at each others' throats, I just didn't understand why Cahir was so hard on him. But then shit like this happened.

"Son, what the fuck?" I leaned back and ran my hand down my face. I knew in business it was always some shit. I had been dealing with this shit a while. But I wasn't in the mood to handle this one.

"I fucked up. He did some foul shit, came at Bella even though he knew that was my shorty. I checked him. I thought he was smart enough to take a hint. But I'm handling the situation."

"You need to get rid of Shay. Bella deserves better than that, and she seems like a real one. Don't end up like me." I looked at my unread messages asking if I could see my daughter and gripped the shit out of my phone in anger.

"I hear you. I'm working on some shit. I don't want to play Bella as number two forever. But I have to make sure Tayari is cool, first."

"I have a lawyer if you need one." He nodded and got up. "Do me a favor before you go. Call Rumor, she wont answer me, and I need to see A'Laya. At this point, if she don't answer, I'm going over there and breaking her neck."

"Yo, you wild as fuck. Maybe you should just give sis some space. She will come back around; she always does. Rumor ain't never going to love another nigga like she loves you and you know it." I just stared at him until he took out his phone. "Yo sis you and Laya good?" He listened to something she said on the other line, and I almost demanded he put it on speaker like a bitch.

"Aight I'm just making sure. Remee been trying to call and see Laya." He paused again, and I could tell he was surprised at whatever she said. "Cool, I will let him know. I'm going to come put the bookshelf together tomorrow, I will bring Bella over to keep you company." He hung up and was quiet.

"The fuck she said?"

"She said A'Laya is busy, and you can get her on Monday from ma." Rumor had never denied me access to my daughter. Laya was my fucking heart. What the fuck bullshit was she on.

"Good looking out." I walked out and left him standing there, a concerned look on his face.

"I see you on some real foul shit, you fucking see me calling you and don't answer your phone but when Sire calls you pick up. You think not letting me see my daughter is cute, but I'm fucking warning you if I don't see her on Monday, I'm fucking you up." I ended the call after leaving the voice message and went to the bar for a drink.

"Give me a double shot of Henny. I tossed the drinks back, enjoying the burn. After an hour, I got up to leave. I sat in my truck and lit a blunt, telling myself to stay away from Rumor's crib. I started to drive and ended up in Jayda's driveway. I knocked on the door, and she opened it, rolling her eyes and sucking her teeth.

"Wow look who decided to show up."

"Where my son at, I didn't come here to do all of that wit ya ass. That's the reason I stay the fuck from round here." I bumped her as I walked in the living room and over to the swing. I swear my son was in this shit every time I came over. Slowly I lifted him out and he waved his tiny hands in my face. It was crazy how much he looked like me. "Sup man, you being good for your mom?" He couldn't respond, just blew some spit bubbles at me.

I chilled with my son for a little while, until he started crying loud as fuck. "Yo, get him a bottle you don't see him crying and shit," I barked at his mom.

"He doesn't use bottles; I need to breastfeed him." She was lying hard as fuck. I've seen him drink from a bottle before. That bitch just wanted to pull out her titties in front of me. She sat down and pulled her maxi dress down then her bra, letting them both pop out at the same time. I watched my sons' tiny lips circle her breasts as he sucked. I sat there staring at him eat until she finally put him over her shoulder to burp him.

She made sure her breasts stayed out as she leaned back and made sure her legs gapped open so I could see she didn't have any panties on. I felt my dick get hard, and I adjusted myself in my jeans. I hadn't had any pussy in a while since Rumor wasn't fucking wit me. Janay got up and put my son down in his playpen before slowly walking towards me. She straddled my lap and stuck her breasts in my face. I wanted to tell her back the fuck up, but I was high as fuck.

Instead of turning her down, I reached in my pocket and grabbed a condom, I pulled my dick out and covered it up. Then slid her down my length. I sat back and watched Jayda fuck me, shorty put a lot of work in, she was moving her body in all the right ways, and before I knew it, I was filling the condom and drifting off to sleep.

SOMEHOW, I FELL INTO THE PATTERN OF FUCKING WITH MY ratchet ass baby moms. I was at her house breaking her down or bussin down her throat every few days. I even let shorty cook me a few meals. I kept asking myself what kind of shit I was on, but without Rumor I felt like nothing really mattered. Jayda was still just something to do with tight holes. Having a daughter, I hated how that shit sounded, I hated the type of nigga I had become. All I did was smoke that purple haze, drink and get money. I been going to see A'Laya at my moms but not taking her home with me like I normally would. I wasn't myself and she didn't need to see that shit.

I sat back and watched the money go through the money counter while Sire and Cahir did the same at their desks. I was enjoying the sound of cash, for once the warehouse was empty, silent. After today this place would be no more, I sold it to a farmer looking to store his tractors and shit. It was time to change operations since Jax was on the loose. My phone buzzed and I groaned inwardly at the texts from Jayda reminding me I was taking her to some whack ass movie today.

"The fuck wrong wit you, look like you got to shit or something," Sire said causing Cahir to snort. I could tell Lo and Grip was trying not to laugh.

"He bout to go on a date with his baby mama," Cahir said giving me a deadly look. I felt like he was more fucked up over the shit wit me and Rumor than I was. "I hope the place is pet friendly, since you bringing out that mutt." He went back to stuffing his money into a duffle bag.

"Nigga please tell me you not bringing Jayda raggedy ass anywhere?" Sire said, a look of shock on his face.

"I swear ya'll stay minding my fucking business. Worry about ya'll own shit. Bella aint going to wait around forever Sire and as for Eternity, shit I see the amount of nigga's that try an get at her daily. Some quality ones, they ready to drop bands on her, and tell the world." Knowing I had pissed them both off I wrapped the last pile in front of me in a rubber band and threw it in my bag. "It's all here," I said referring to the half a mill, that was my cut from this week's profits. "I'm out," I said dapping them up and heading for the door.

My first stop was my house, so I could put money in my safe. I threw the four hundred thousand in the safe in the basement floor and headed out. I sat parked across from Rumors condo waiting for her to leave. I watched as she grabbed my daughters' hand and carefully put her in her booster seat. Baby girl had on her little dance outfit. My mom told me that's why Laya had been busy on the weekends. She was taking a dance class. Ru always had my shorty in something and appreciated her for being such a good mom. Once they pulled off, I went inside, the scent of Rumors perfume made me want to just stay in this bitch and wait on her to come home. Beg her to make this shit right. Instead I opened her safe in the closet and threw the last hundred thousand in there.

I doubted she even looked inside this bitch, the way the money was just stacking up. She had enough of my money on the books that she really didn't have to reach for the cash I provided. It was just in case though. The reality was I sold drugs for a living and at any moment this shit could end. And I never wanted Ru or Laya to worry about shit. I smiled when I noticed she still had a picture of me, her and Laya on her bedside table. Maybe she still loved me, a little bit.

I drove to Jayda's house hoping to get this little movie shit out the way. I wasn't into taking bitches on dates and shit, unless it was Ru. I was only taking her today because I was way to rough when I fucked her last week and she had a nigga feeling bad. I pulled up and blew the horn, causing her to poke her head out of the door and give me a dirty look. I rolled down the window. "You ready or we not going because I got other shit to do. Matter of fact drive your own shit and just meet me there," I said pulling off, since she couldn't be fucking ready when she knew I was on the way. Tinsletown was around the corner from her spot, so I made it there in good timing and parked my car. She was talking shit when I left but I noticed how fast she rolled up to the theater.

We walked in together and Jayda tried grabbing my hand, I gave her the look of death. "Babe what do you want to see," she asked, and I looked at her sideways.

"The fuck you mean what I want to see. You didn't know what you came here to watch after you begged me to bring you every fucking day this week?" I walked to the ticket counter not even paying her ass any attention. She was about to watch whatever the fuck was playing right now. Dumb bitch.

"Daddy," I heard someone shout and my heart dropped. It couldn't be, but as I slowly turned around A'Laya was running my way. Her mother followed with a look of devastation on her face. I picked my baby up and she was all smiles. She had no idea that the adults around her were anything but happy. "Did you come to see the movie with us? We are going to watch the one with the fire truck and the dog. It's funny, you will like it."

"A'Laya get over here now," Rumor snapped causing my daughter to frown.

"But mommy, I'm with my daddy. I miss him." Laya said, her voice wobbling.

"Yo, don't be snapping on my shorty like you crazy." I heard Jayda suck her teeth from behind me. "You can go," I said dismissing her with a look.

"Nigga fuck you and your daughter. You think you can play me for a kid that aint even yours."

"Daddy why did she say I'm not yours? I'm not your daughter?" A'Laya asked, her head titled to the side and tears pooling in her eyes.

"She capping baby girl, you know I'm your only daddy and your my only daughter." I wiped the tears from her eyes and kissed her gently on the cheek. "Now go with mommy and get our tickets and daddy will be right there." She was back to smiling and Jayda had better be happy she was. I handed her a hundred-dollar bill and she skipped over to her mother.

"Here mommy, buy our tickets. Daddies too," she said, and I winked at her.

I turned and caught up with Jayda at the door, I snatched her by the back of her neck causing a few people to gasp. "Bitch, I told you about fucking with my daughter right." She slowly nodded her head, unable to speak with the pressure I was putting on her neck. "If it aint about Javani, don't hit my line. I don't care if you're on fire, bitch, do not call me. I will be picking my son up soon. You will never get another pass concerning my daughter, so don't think you will." I let her go and she ran up out of the building coughing and shit.

I went to the line and caught up to Rumor. She gave me the loo of death as I picked Laya back up. "You can leave Remee or go back to your woman. We don't need you here." Her voice was cold, and her eyes even worse. I didn't say shit just stood there until we got tickets. I let Laya pay and she enjoyed that, especially the part where she got to keep the change. She was shoving it in her little purse.

"I want popcorn, candy and a slushie." She said skipping towards the concession. Her mother must have been waiting on the opportunity to get me somewhat alone.

"Nigga, I said leave. Me and my daughter don't need shit from you, definitely not your presence. Not even your money. I work." I didn't even know what to say, I had hurt her and this time it was bad.

"I know I hurt you again, I know you tired of me saying I'm sorry. Just don't try and take me out of Laya's life. I will leave you alone if that's what you want. You got that, but I can't lose her."

RUMOR

I sat in my car silently counting to ten praying I didn't run into this nigga. Remee had me fucked up and he had been doing the right thing by avoiding me since the movie incident. I was sure he didn't decide to come to his mother's house today expecting to run into me. As a matter of fact, I was the one at fault. I left work three hours early so I could take Laya to the museum. I had been moping around the house and she was starting to pick up on my mood. I let myself in and walked to the back hoping to find her and Miss Layla in the kitchen. But as soon as I got closer, I heard what sounded like her crying.

"A'Remee I just don't understand. I feel like you're not trying. Like you don't care if I see my grandson or not. I have held him twice in my life. I ask you to bring him over almost every day. You barely respond. Don't you love your son?"

"You don't understand ma," he said, his voice sounding strained. "She won't let me get my son unless I don't see my daughter. He can't come here unless A'Laya can no longer come here. Am I supposed to just ignore my daughter or turn my back on her for him? That's what the fuck you want me to do?

That's what you want to do?" He was damn near shouting now, the anger and frustration clear in his tone.

"That's ridiculous Remee and you know it. You make all these fools in the streets do what you want but when it comes to this one female you have allowed her to literally ruin your life and hold your son hostage. And now this shit is affecting me." The pain in her voice made me feel like shit. Miss Layla was hurting because of me and my daughter. "Remee be honest, do you even care about your son?"

"What the hell kind of question is that? He is still being taken care of so hell yea I give a fuck about him. Ma, I don't know what you want from me. Its not the same as with Laya. He's my kid, I care about him. But the connection is hard. When I see him it hurts, it fucks with me. It reminds me of Junior, and all the shit I fucked up, all the shit I lost. There's no joy in that. Everybody on me about bringing Javani around, but unless you want me to kill his mother, I don't have any other solutions. Because that's exactly how I handle these fools in the streets."

"Come on ma, don't cry. I will figure it out." I peeked around the corner and saw him hugging his mom. The look on her face caused my eyes to tear up. Miss Layla had been good to me, sacrificed enough for me. When I looked at the bigger picture her and Remee where hurting because I was around. And even though I hated this nigga, I loved him too. I knew what my next move was, one I should have made a long time ago.

I ran up the stairs and packed up some of A'Laya's stuff, I swear she acted like she lived here too. "Mommy, you're here," she said dancing into the room, a big smile on her face. I knew the shit I was about to do would hurt her, but kids bounced back, they were resilient as fuck and she would be ok. Javani deserved a father and a loving family, none of this was his fault. He was an innocent child.

"Yes, I am, now let's go. Make sure you bring La La." I said pointing to her stuffed lamb. She got that as a baby from her

Uncle Sire and didn't leave home with out. If she left it anywhere there was nothing but tears, sleepless nights and aggravation.

"Hey Rumor, when did you get here?" Miss Layla asked standing in the doorway, startling me.

"A few minutes ago," I said. I was trying my hardest not to look sad. I would miss her. "I have to go though. We have to go." I was stuttering and I was sure I sounded crazy. "Laya give Mi Mi a hug goodbye."

"Rumor are you ok?" She asked as she picked up my baby and kissed her cheeks. "I can keep her until tomorrow night or even the weekend if you need a break. You're here early did something happen at work?" She reached out and touched my hand and I started to cry. I had to pull myself together because I knew she would call Remee back here if she thought I was in trouble.

"I'm good I promise." I lied wiping my tears. "I just had a bad day at work and want to go home and crawl in my bed with my baby and cuddle. I'm sure tomorrow will be better."

"Ok Rumor but promise you will tell me if something is wrong. You can stay here if you want? I wouldn't mind the company?"

"Thank you but no, I just want to go home. Come on Laya." I grabbed her little duffel bag and held out my hands for her.

"Well ok, I will see you tomorrow baby. Mi Mi loves you." Laya kissed the only grandma she ever knew and waved.

As we walked down the stairs, I knew I had to tell her something, because A'Laya wouldn't be coming over tomorrow. "Miss Layla, she won't be here the rest of the week. I'm going to be home and I been looking into daycare for her. You shouldn't have to baby sit all the time. Just be grandma and enjoy her company." She started to say something, but I hurried to kiss her on the cheek and walk out the door. I hated this shit, but I had to do what was best for everyone.

I stopped at my car and grabbed the stuff I needed, the whole time I kept my eye on the house making sure Miss Layla wasn't paying attention. Throwing my keys inside I closed the door and me and A'Laya walked to the end of the driveway to wait on an uber.

"Mommy why aren't we getting in our car. I want to play with my toys," Laya whined as we climbed in back of the Chevy Malibu that came to pick us up.

"Daddy is taking it to be fixed, so we are taking an Uber, we will be home soon, and you can play with your toys." My answer seemed to satisfy her, she smiled and sat back for the ride. We made it home and as soon as I walked through the door Remee was calling. I rejected him a few times then blocked him. My hands started sweating and I jumped into action. I felt like my window to pack my shit and get the fuck out of here was closing.

I grabbed some apple slices, peanut butter and a juice box then set them on the table. "Laya, come have a snack baby so mommy can pack our clothes. We are going on a trip." My daughter titled her head and looked at me, for a second I swore her eyes appeared almost golden. I was losing my fucking mind.

"No trip. I want my daddy." She crossed her arms over her small chest, and I knew by the end of this day I was going to have a headache. Deciding to ignore her for now I ran upstairs and grabbed two suitcases. I grabbed mostly stuff for Laya. I could do without. An hour later I was sweating and just wanted to crawl into my comfy king size bed, even if it was only for one last night, but I knew if I did, I wouldn't leave. I opened the safe and placed all of my cards in there except the one for my credit union. My paychecks went into that account, and I would need every penny going forward where I was headed. I took out exactly four five hundred dollars in cash, baffled at the stacks of hundreds that were in there. I rarely used my safe, but I could see Remee had been adding money without my knowledge.

Shit like this made me confused about how to feel where Remee was concerned. Was it that easy for him to just hand over money? Money that he risked his life for. Or was that love? I just wasn't sure. The lines were blurred, because money really didn't equal love. I remembered being poor, and I couldn't have imagined not having shit. But still giving someone else some of the little I did have. Wasn't that what parents did for their kids and that was the purset form of love. When Remee just started getting money he took care of me, as many other bitches that he fucked that was something he never did for them. At least until Jayda came along. Thinking about her had me closing the safe and proceeding with my plan.

The whole time I showered, got dressed in a sweat suit and got Laya ready, I felt like I was robbing a bank. My hands were shaking, and I was sweating. I should have drove my car home and parked it. Leaving it there had Miss Layla calling and texting me, asking questions. I knew once I started ignoring Amira's calls it was time to get the fuck on. My phone buzzed, the message this time from my ride. Seeing his name caused my stomach to cramp, I said a quick prayer that this was the right decision.

"Come on A'Laya we are going bye-bye." She glared but placed her tiny hand in mine as I juggled the suitcases and a bookbag. The black BMW was sitting on the street still running, the trunk popped as I got closer, but he didn't get out to help. Throwing my stuff inside I closed the trunk, looking around I felt paranoid, if Remee showed up right now it would be a blood bath.

After I buckled A'Laya in the back I went to slide in next to her. "Naw, sit your ass up front Rumor. You too good to sit up here with me," he said, laughing. The laugh sounded off, but I needed his help, so I brushed it off. Gently I closed the door and got in the front. We drove in silence, Laya had her tablet and headphones to occupy her and I had my thoughts. Finally, we got close to my destination.

"So, what do I get for all of this help I'm giving you?" He said turning into an alley.

"A thank you, shit what else you want," I snapped. I was trying to sound unbothered, but that wasn't how I felt. His big hand gripped my leg and he sneered at me.

"Naw Rumor, you owe me a lot more than that, and I came to collect."

ETERNITY

I thought after seeing Cahir at the block party he would have kept his distance, but instead it was the total opposite. He was here most nights I worked, and instead of watching from the corner he would sit right at the bar staring in my face, just like he was now. I couldn't wait to get off, he made me uncomfortable. I couldn't read him, honestly I never could and that fucked with my head. Finally, it was two and my shift was over. I didn't stay a moment longer than I had to, and not just because of stalking ass Cahir. But because my manager Tatianna was a true bitch and my hand was itching to slap the shit out of her. Today she intentionally spilled a drink all over me and now I was sticky as fuck and my shirt was still damp. If I didn't need my job and didn't respect Remee's establishment I would have smashed her face into the fucking bar.

Grabbing my bag and a jacket, I walked outside to my car. "Yo Tee, let me talk to you for a minute?" Cahir said from behind me causing me to damn near jump out my skin.

"Damn, announce yourself, what the fuck. It's bad enough you stay on my job like you working in this bitch. Just staring and watching me, you were already giving me serial killer vibes and now your creeping up on me as I get into my car." He didn't say shit but moved so he was blocking the door to my car.

"You done?" he asked, arms folded across his chest as he leaned against my whip.

"No, but you are. I don't want to talk to you. I've already had a fucked-up day so all I need is for you to move so I can go home." He still stood there, like nothing I said mattered. A cocky smirk on his face. I wanted to kick him in his kneecaps or better yet his dick. My mind flashed back to the day at the park when he was damn near raping that girls' mouth. I guess he really was into rough sex. I didn't know if that made me special or the worst fuck he ever had. Maybe I wasn't even worth the effort, at this point I no longer believed that anything we had ever done meant anything. At least to him. None of it was real.

"Damn, you thinking hard as fuck. If you would have just agreed to talk to me, you could have been on your way by now." He reached out and touched me, it was gentle and reminded me of the time we had spent together. "Just come here for one second. Please." Hearing him say that shit sounded painful as fuck. I knew he didn't use that word often, or probably ever. I walked closer to him and he pulled me into his arms. I didn't know what the fuck I was doing, I told myself stop but I still found myself resting my head on his chest. I inhaled his Gucci Guilty cologne and felt at ease and I should have felt anything but.

"I miss you Tee," he said so low I barely caught it. But one thing for sure I didn't believe it.

"Ransom, how the fuck you miss me, you made it clear I wasn't shit to you, but a bad fuck. I can't even say you missed the sex. What you miss, hurting my feelings?"

"Yo stop calling me that shit, you know my fucking name. And I know you don't believe me, I fucked up ma. I'm sorry. I wish I could say I never meant to hurt you but shit I did. But one thing for sure, what I said was bullshit. We both know your pussy good as fuck." I smiled a little because I knew my shit was solid. I wanted to be happy he was honest, but the fact that he admitted to hurting me intentionally had me side eyeing the fuck out of him.

"Ok so you lied when you said that shit and you meant to hurt me. Why would you do something like that?"

"Yo I aint trying to talk in the middle the parking lot. I meant I need to sit down and talk to you shorty."

"You said just give you a minute and I could be on my way. I gave you more than that, now move. I'm going home, my clothes are wet, my day has been fucked up and you are only adding to the aggravation." His grip on me tightened and I sighed.

"Aight, bet, you go home, I'm going to see you there." He let me go and I didn't have the energy to tell him stay where the fuck he was at. I had butterflies in my stomach the whole drive home, even though I didn't see Cahir's car behind me. Maybe he said fuck it and found some other female's feelings to fuck wit. I parked in front of my place and just sat there for a few minutes. I was damn near too tired to get out of the car, and another part of me hoped Cahir was going to pull up next to me. After twenty minutes I realized he wasn't coming. I leaned over to grab my purse but jumped when I heard a crash. The glass to my driver side window was all over me and the seat. I felt a strong hand grip my throat and I couldn't breathe.

I knew this wasn't Cahir, he wouldn't do no shit like this. Was I being robbed? I should have come home and went right the fuck inside. It was a little late for regrets now. The hand drug me closer to the window, until a face came into view. My heart stopped when I saw him, it was like I was looking into the face of a ghost.

"Yea bitch you never thought you would see me again. But I found you," he sneered, his voice loud in the quiet night. I never thought this would be my life again, but they always say you can't outrun your demons. And they were right, because mine was standing in front of me.

CAHIR

*T*his sleep was about to be good as a bitch after being on the road for weeks. I never did out of town trips that lasted this long. But since I was avoiding Eternity, I stayed way longer than needed. Yea I apologized, but that didn't change the fact that I couldn't be with shorty. I just didn't want her to hate me any more than she already did. So, I damn near watched a whole batch of coke grow from the ground up just to keep myself out of New York and out of her bed. Too bad that shit didn't keep shorty out of my mind. I even hit Sire up a few times to see how she was doing. And as tired as I was, I knew I would be inside of club Remi` tonight just so I could look in her face. As soon as I finally fell into a deep sleep, I felt a presence standing over me. Grabbing my gun, I put one in the chamber only to see my aunt pacing the room, stopping next to my bed every few minutes. Jesus, I forgot she had a fucking key from when I first moved in this spot. Good thing I didn't bring bitches back here or she would have been looking at ass naked broads.

"You know Cahir I don't know why the hell you have this big ass house and its empty. No girlfriend, no kids. Nothing. And you know what else? I wonder why you little niggas have phones only for no one to answer." She stopped in front of me, her pretty wrinkle-free face balled up. She had her hands on her hips, and she totally disregarded my gun that was now sitting on the bedside table next to me. Shaking her head in disappointment, I knew this was far from over. I low key let my eyes glance at my phones only to see the missed calls from her and a few others. But nothing from Eternity.

"Let me tell you something I haven't seen my granddaughter in two weeks. Remee's ass is nowhere to be found. SOMEONE needs to find my granddaughter, now!" I looked at her confused as fuck. She barely saw Sire's daughter to begin with, and A'Laya was with her every day. My aunt barely even raised her voice and she was standing here going in like it was my kid missing.

"Auntie, what's up? Shay on some bullshit wit Tayari?" I prayed that hoe didn't disrespect my aunt because she would be crippled for life fucking wit me.

"Cahir, get up and take me to wherever the hell A'Remee is hiding out. I don't know what that boy did now, but I haven't seen A'Laya in weeks. Rumor left her car at my house, the keys were inside and she has not been back since. She came in that day crying, saying something about Laya going to daycare and then was just gone." I jumped up and went to find some clothes. Hearing that Rumor was missing had me moving my ass. Rumor been around as long as I can remember and had my cousin's back more than that nigga deserved. At the end of the day, she was family.

"Meet me in the car," my aunt called over her shoulder as she exited my room. "And put a picture up or something, this house looks sad." I laughed low, she didn't give up, shit all of Laya's and Tayari's photos were on my refrigerator. Aside from that who the fuck was I putting pictures up of? For a second, I imagined pictures of Eternity and her son framed up on the walls. That bitch had voodoo pussy, that's the what the fuck it was.

Got my head all fucked up. I threw on some Balmain jeans and a Versace red and black hoodie. Black Timberlands on my feet I didn't bother with any jewelry aside from the diamond earrings I already had in and the Rolex I slid on.

I made it outside to see my Porsche Cayenne out of the garage and sitting idle. If it were anyone but my aunt, I would have been tight. "I guess I'm driving," I said as I got in talking shit. She gave me the look of death as I focused on getting to the club where I knew Remee's ass was. If this nigga would have just answered his phone, I would still be fucking sleeping. When we pulled in the parking lot, I parked right next to Remee's Range Rover and Amira's Benz. I guess we weren't the only people looking for Rumor.

"Yea I should have known he would be here, hiding," my aunt sassed as I helped her out of the truck. "Hopefully, Amira already has the information I need so my baby can hurry back to me." I just nodded, not really wanting to get involved in the Remee and Rumor drama. I spoke my peace on they shit a long time ago after she almost lost her life. So, at this point, as long as she and Laya were straight, I didn't give a fuck what was going on.

Being that it was the daytime the club wasn't opened to the public. I knew that some of the staff would be there doing set up and cleaning. But when I walked in, I didn't expect to see her standing at the bar. Little man was with her, pulling on her hand impatiently. I wondered what she was doing here in the daytime and with her son. I held back so she wouldn't notice me right away. Almost instinctively my aunt stayed next to me waiting to see what I was doing.

Eternity leaned closer to the bar. "Tatianna, I don't know why the fuck you're giving me a hard time, I just came for my check. Please hurry up because I have an Uber outside waiting on me." Her voice sounded squeaky like she was trying not to cry. What the fuck was she doing in an Uber. Amira came downstairs and stood next to my aunt, and for some reason, I felt like all eyes were on me. They didn't say a word just stood there watching me, watching her. I was sure this wasn't what any of us came here for. They were here to dig into Remee's business, not mine.

"And I already told you Eternity I don't give my employees their paychecks until they clock in for their shifts on Friday nights. Now my suggestion to you is that you come back, on time for your shift if you would like your check." Tatianna was smirking and shit, laughing right in shorty face.

"That's the rule, right? So why the hell Roxie just got her check, and she isn't clocked in yet? I guess it's just the rule for me!" Before I could step in Tatianna clapped back.

"Listen Eternity, I know you are used to special treatment since your fucking the owner's friends and shit, but this ain't that. You're no longer a bottle girl, and I don't' care who you are spreading your legs for. So again, in case you didn't understand you will get your check tonight when you are here working. If this doesn't work for you, quit."

"Yo Tatianna, you got ten seconds to get shorty her check. If she walks in here on Wednesday from now on and wants her fucking check, you better have it ready. If you ever say some shit like that to her again you won't have to worry about your job, but you will have to worry about your life," I hissed as I calmly walked close enough for her to see I wasn't playing. "And for the record, she ain't fucking the owner's friends bitch. She's fucking me." I heard Tee gasp next to me. Yea I wanted to keep our shit low when we were fucking around, and we hadn't fucked in months. But I wasn't about to let anyone disrespect her again. I let that shit get too far the last time and I walked away from shorty because of it.

I turned to Tee, my eyes roaming her body. Her jeans were hugging all her curves, and the bright green and black long-sleeved shirt made her brown eyes lighter. She looked like she had gotten thicker over the past few weeks, and I wondered if she was carrying my baby. I swear I was never careful running up in her shit. For the first time in my life, the thought of a woman walking around with my seed had me intrigued. Slowly I walked up behind Eternity and wrapped my arms around her. I let my hands brush over her still flat belly and felt disappointment wash over me. I wanted to suck on her neck, then kiss her soft lips but too many people were here, including her son.

Tatianna came and handed her the check, her face was turned up, but her hand was shaking, so I knew that bitch got the point. "Thank you," Eternity said as she shrugged me off of her and turned to leave. She never even acknowledged I was standing there.

"Mommy, I'm so hungry, can we eat now?" Her son asked, a pleading look on his face.

"Cassian, we will eat once we get home," she said, running her hand over the top of his head, trying to comfort him, I guess. As soon as she said his name, I noticed the look on my aunt and cousin's faces. *Fuck.*

All eyes were on Eternity as my aunt found her voice. "Cahir is that your son?" She damn near yelled, causing Tatianna to drop a glass on the floor in shock. She was in my face before I could react. "I just begged you for more grandbabies to spoil this morning. We just talked about that big empty house and all this time you have a son right under my nose?" She punched me hard as fuck in my chest. Dead ass if she wasn't like a mom to me I would have snapped her fucking neck. Stepping in front of Eternity and Cassian. "He is so cute," she gushed hugging him to her.

"I'm sorry ma'am, this isn't Cahir's son. I'm not sure why you would think that. I barely know Cahir. This is a misunderstanding." Hearing her tell my aunt that she barely knew me hurt my heart. I didn't know why. I was the one who didn't want anyone to know we were fucking, and she was just sticking to the plan.

Eternity gently pulled Cassian back towards her and looked at me with fear in her eyes. Damn it was that deep, she thought I was going to wile her up if my aunt found out we had messed around. I was about to say fuck it because I didn't want my family to think she was just some pop off. She meant more than that to me.

"I'm sorry I didn't get your name. I'm Cahir's aunt Layla, and I raised that boy. You definitely know him. I have never seen him come to any woman's rescue who wasn't family. Aside from the fact you are using his government name. Plus, I can see the way he been looking at you since we walked in here. So, what I would love to do is get to know the woman who has broken through my nephew's cold exterior. And I'm curious to know why your son's name is Cahir's middle name."

"Umm-hmm," Tatianna mumbled from behind the bar.

"I'm sorry little girl don't you have a job to do?" My aunt said addressing her. She slowly nodded. "Well get to your fucking job then scram." I chuckled. I swear this was the grandma who baked cookies and shit, but today she was all the way live. She looked back at Eternity, still waiting on an answer. I knew I wasn't shit, but I would never turn my back on my kid if I had one—especially not one that Tee gave me.

Shit, I knew her son's name the first day I met her in the McDonalds. I just never told her that was my middle name. I kind of liked that her son and I shared that, and I kept it to myself. Eternity was glaring at me now, and I knew she was annoyed I didn't tell her. "Well umm, it was nice to meet you Miss Layla. I really have to go; I have an uber waiting. I'm sorry, I truly didn't know that was Cahir's middle name. Coincidence, I guess. I'm sure my son would have been super blessed to have an Aunt like you in his life," she said before grabbing Cassian's hand and damn near running towards the door.

"Tee, come here," I commanded, she kept walking but

Cassian stopped causing her to halt in her tracks. "Mommy, Cahir is calling you and I didn't get to say hi," he stated.

I walked over and dapped him up. "You been good for mommy," I asked.

"Yes sir," he replied grinning.

Slowly Eternity, turned towards me, her face filled with frustration. "Don't do that ma," I said, pulling her closer to me. I had missed her so fucking much I couldn't hold back. I looked down at her for a second just taking in her beauty, before I lowered my head and gently kissed her. "The fuck you in an Uber for, where your car at? Tell that nigga you good."

"Not that it's any of your business, but I need to have the window fixed before it will pass inspection. And no, I ain't telling my ride to leave. He was nice enough to wait when they not even supposed to that."

I nodded slowly before going outside before her. I saw the silver Nissan Altima and the nigga sitting inside smoking a blunt, music loud. Knocking on the window hard as fuck he dropped that shit in his lap and jumped. He just stared at me eyes wide open, dumb as fuck. I opened the door and snatched his ass out of the car. "Mother fucker what you out here doing waiting on my fucking girl? You not supposed to be waiting on people, right?" He shook his head like a naughty child. "Talk up bitch," I said, hitting him with my gun. I didn't even realize I had it in my hand.

"No, I was just trying to be nice. She begged me, and I wanted to help a pretty girl out." He got out stuttering and shit.

"A pretty girl, right?" I hit his ass again. "Nah, you thought you were going to wait on my woman so you could fuck her after the ride! Guess what mahfucker you will never get her pussy, that shit belongs to me. Now get in your fucking car and pull off before I murk yo retarded ass." I threw him back in the seat, and he was pulling off before the door was closed. I was seething mad. I felt like a fucking animal, someone with no

126

control. The thought of another nigga talking to Eternity, touching her had me going crazy.

"Now how the fuck am I supposed to get home Cahir!" She barked from the doorway of the club. I noticed my aunt had her son sitting at one of the tables as she bossed one of the workers around. A few seconds later he came out with a soda and some chips for little man.

"I will drive you," Amira volunteered a grin on her face.

"Hell, no you won't nosey ass. You need to go and find your damn friend and tell her if I don't see my daughter by the end of today, I'm fucking her up." Remee spat, cutting short her dreams of getting in my business.

"Fine, it was nice to see you again Eternity," she said, smiling her way, before stomping out of the club.

"Amira hold up, a nigga needs a ride," I said interrupting her grand exit. I turned to Tee and handed her the keys to my Porsche. "Don't say no dumb shit to piss me off either. I don't want you out here catching rides and shit. Especially with him," I said, motioning towards her son. "That shit ain't safe, and I don't have time to be worrying." I went into my pockets and gave her some cash. "Go buy him something to eat before you do whatever else you got to do. Next time you got a fucking problem pick up the phone and call. Stop being hardheaded." She tried to hand me my keys and money back, but I ignored her. If she kept it up, I was breaking her fucking wrist.

"Auntie let's roll unless you're staying here." She got up walking Cassian over to us reluctantly. "Aight little nigga, take care of your mom ya heard?" I dapped him up, and he smiled at me.

"Yes sir," he responded, moving closer to his mom. He was looking at me like he was figuring some shit out.

"Come on. I'm walking ya'll out." My aunt and cousin talked and giggled the whole way to Amira's whip while I walked them to the truck. Opening the backdoor, I helped Cassian buckle up and handed him the headphones that went to the TV I had back there. It was only one kid DVD in there. It was some Pets shit Laya always wanted to watch, so I turned it on for him.

"Mommy, there is a TV," he shouted excitedly to which she rolled her eyes.

"Don't get used to it," she warned as I closed the door.

"Mane don't tell him that shit. This ya whip now, so he better get used to it. She laughed so hard tears came out her eyes.

"Really? You just giving me a sixty-thousand-dollar truck? I mean, I know my pussy good but not that good." I leaned her against the truck and played in her ponytail. I loved how silky her hair was.

"Hell yea your pussy is that good. Worth way more than a fucking truck. You could run a nigga pockets with that shit." I meant that shit too, I was just shocked as fuck I said it out loud.

The sun came out and shined on her face. The minute I saw the bruises on her neck I felt like someone had hit me. "You Tee, what the fuck happened to your neck." I asked as I gently pushed her body agains the car with mine. She wasn't going any fucking where until I got an answer.

She dropped her head, "nothing Ransom," I have to go. I will drop your truck off here later when I start my shift." She tried to wiggle away from me, but I gently grabbed her hair and tilted her head to the side. Clear as day I could see the fingerprints on her neck, the deep purple bruises were deeper on the left side.

"Eternity, a nigga putting his hands on you?"

REMEE

I sat in Rumor's couch, my head in my hands. I had looked everywhere for Ru and my daughter and I couldn't find them. The condo was damn near untouched except some missing clothes and shoes. Her Patek and Rolex were still in their place, hell all her jewelry was except the diamond heart necklace I copped her back in the day. She wore that shit regular and I guess she couldn't leave it behind. Maybe she was kidnapped. I had enemies, I wanted to say most wouldn't bring a man's family into this shit, but you never knew, these niggas now a days would kill their own mother for a few dollars. It could have been that fucking Jax, even though his beef was with Sire. Maybe he saw my shorty somewhere and took it as an opportunity.

I opened the safe and all the money was there, her credit cards and bank cards next to them. Something wasn't right, why the fuck would Ru leave with no money, and worse with my daughter. I picked up the phone and dialed Sire's number. "Sup," he answered sounding half asleep.

"Yo, you heard from Rumor?"

"Naw, she pissed at you again?"

"Ask ya shorty if she talked to her," I demanded.

"You know she don't fuck wit my girl like that."

"Nigga, ya other shorty. The burger king chick don't fucking play stupid, this shit is serious. My girl is missing."

"Last I knew nigga your girl was Jayda, you was spending nights, fucking and even enjoying her home cooked meals. So, I'm not sure when you started worrying about Rumor again."

"Mane you a hardheaded ass nigga, I swear. It's like you not listening. it's like you not fucking hearing me. First of all don't worry about what me and Jayda have going on. I'm grown and if I want to fuck my baby mom's I will. Ma, told me Rumor and Laya aint been around the whole fucking time I been out of town. She hasn't answered her phone for even Amira. Her truck was parked here, she left her car at my mom's and all her money and cards still at the fucking crib. Her and Laya are nowhere to be found."

"A'Laya aint wit ma? Yo I'm about to hit you back." He hung up, getting the shit now. I don't know why I thought that Bella knew where Rumor was, but at this point I was getting desperate. Something about this shit was starting to feel wrong as fuck. I left the condo and rode around for a while. I went to her job and they said she was out sick. A lot of this shit looked like she ran away, but something inside of me wouldn't allow myself to believe that. She wouldn't just leave me.

I drove to bitch ass Jordan's spot. I always kept tabs on him in case he ever tried to come near my daughter. If he did that was his fucking life. His car was parked outside so I knew he was home. If I found out he had anything to do with this I wasn't sparing his life. I stopped to look in his whip, and what I saw caused my blood to run cold. La La was on the floor of the back seat. I smashed his window in causing neighbors to look out of their windows. Nosey mahfuckers. I didn't care who was watching, I scoured his shit and found Rumors heart necklace broken in the front seat and drops of blood on the brown leather.

I rushed up to the door and didn't bother knocking, I kicked that shit in. Jordan was in the living room hiding behind the couch like the bitch that he was. "Man, listen, she wanted me to get her, I just dropped her off. I swear." I looked around his place and spotted some of that thick ass silver tape. I grabbed it and taped his mouth shut. I didn't want to hear shit else he had to say. Not yet at least.

"I only have one fucking question, they here?" He shook his head no. His eyes wide with fear. I still checked the place thoroughly, I even pried up a few floorboards making sure he wasn't on no serial killer shit. But there was no one else here. "We going for a fucking ride," I growled as I grabbed him up. Once we made it outside, I threw him in my trunk and sped the fuck off. I had a new spot to take people and torture them, and that was were I was headed. I kept glancing at the seat next to me where I had put my baby girl's stuffed animal. I felt in that moment I was truly going crazy. If I didn't see my daughter again, they might as well just kill me, because I would never be the same.

Thinking about Laya had me hitting the gas harder. I was barely paying attention to my driving until I heard the siren behind me. But by then it was too late. I was doing sixty in a ninety and now I had two choices, either pull over with a nigga bound and gagged in the trunk. Or go on a high-speed chase. Fuck!

SIRE

I looked at Bella as she arched her back and felt my dick get even harder. Smacking her ass a few times I spread her pussy lips with my fingers and just watched the wetness. Instead of sliding inside like I wanted to I kissed her down her back and then I slowly made my way to her treasure. I had never been one to eat a lot of pussy until I met Bella. Her shit was sweet, like I was eating sugar. I bit her clit lightly and she called my name into the blankets. "That's right Bella, get that pussy wet for ya nigga," I said causing her to snake her hand around and start fingering herself. That shit was hot as fuck, especially when she pulled them out and slipped them in my mouth.

"Yo you sexy as fuck," I muttered as I grabbed her ass and pushed my way inside. I swear shorty had some snap back pussy, because even with me busting her down on the regular it seemed like I still had to force my way inside. It only took a few minutes before she was slamming her body back against mine and my dick was able to get deeper inside. I loved seeing her cream all over me, it made me go harder.

"Sire, pull out," she said but I ignored her and when she

came, I nut inside of her. It was stupid as fuck, since I had a woman. But I loved feeling her raw, and her pussy was so good I just couldn't stop myself. "I aint having any more fucking kids so you need to stop that shit." She was annoyed and I knew I was on thin ice as it was. I made sure I took that friend shit I promised her and turned it back into something more. I missed the way she felt, not just her pussy but her lips, her touch. Bella was my drug.

"Your phone has been going off," she said, and I jumped to look at who was calling. With Rumor still missing shit had been hectic. But at least tonight I was taking care of Jax, one less problem. I had five missed calls from Shay and a nine one one text.

"Sire did you hear what I said? These niggas followed me while I had our daughter in the car. They shot at us and ran me off the road. You need to get here now. I was so scared." I barely understood everything Shay was saying because she was hysterical. I didn't even want to hang up, I needed to know her and Tayari where good.

"Yo calm down, send me your location, I'm on the way."

"I'm home now nigga, I been calling you for over a damn hour!" Shay was snapping and for the first time she had all rights to be mad.

"Aight, just stay the fuck inside, I'm headed that way." I hit mute at the same time I jumped out of bed. *Fuck.* With Rumor missing I should have been paying more attention to my family and their safety. I was so hooked on laying up with Bella, I forgot about Shay, which really meant I forgot about Tayari. This was why I never wanted to be out here fucking with a bunch of chicks. It wasn't fair, someone always suffered and usually someone got hurt. Had my daughter been hurt today I would have never forgiven myself.

"Yo Bells, I got to go. I'm sorry ma." I had my pants buckled and threw my hoodie on, not even taking the time to put on my t-shirt. She didn't respond, so I glanced her way. I hated the look she had on her face the tears that sat perched on her cheeks ready to drop. We had plans today, some cooking show that came on tv was doing a live taping here and I had copped us some VIP tickets. It was the first thing shorty had ever asked me for and I was happy as fuck to give it to her. Except now I had to snatch it away from her.

"I will make it up to you I promise. I just, I gotta go. Some shit went down wit my girl." Her face turned cold and she looked away from me. "Come on Bella don't do that shit ma," I pleaded as I grabbed my keys.

"Sire, just leave."

* * *

I PULLED UP AT MY HOUSE FIFTEEN MINUTES LATER, AND I WAS thirty minutes away. I was lost on the fact that Shay's G-Wagon was parked in the driveway since she was crying about being ran the fuck off the road. I surveyed the front and noticed a broken light and a dent on the driver's side door. She made it seem like her shit was totaled. I didn't see one bullet hole so either these niggas were a bad shot, or she was exaggerating. I opened the front door and didn't see her or my daughter. For some reason I didn't announce myself, I silently walked up the stairs until I got closer to our bedroom. I stopped myself from going in when I heard her laughing. The fuck was she laughing for and some nigga's damn near blew her top off.

"Girl, he fell for that shit, just like you said he would. You should have heard how he sounded. I never heard him that concerned over something involving me. I bet he left that bitch high and dry and he's going to feel guilty enough to leave her alone going forward." I couldn't believe this bitch, she had really played the fuck out of my ass. "Jayda, I have to go, he's gonna be here soon." She paused and I could tell her reckless ass homegirl was offering more advice. "Hell, no I aint punching myself in the face, I will call you later after I fuck him to sleep."

I let her sit there on the bed for a minute, a wide smile on her face while I just watched from the doorway. This bitch was the worst kind of female and I was thinking of places to hide her body. This shit was foul, all because she wanted me to stop fucking with Bella. "Daddy," Tayari called out as she left her room and walked down the hall. It caused her mother to look up, the smile she had long gone.

I picked my baby up and kissed her. I checked her over just in case her mother tried some other dumb shit to make me believe her story. Luckily Tayari didn't have a scratch on her. "Go play in your room baby," I said setting my daughter down. I stepped into the room and for the first time since I met her Shay had a look of raw fear on her face.

"You don't understand, I was trying to save us, she was ruining our family." She was crying now, real tears, the ones that caused your body to shake and your chest to heave. But I didn't care, her tears didn't move me in the least.

"Shay, you are a scandalous bitch and I regret the day I met you and I definitely regret the day I ran in your hoe ass and got you pregnant." She tried to say something as she slithered off the bed and headed my way. "Don't say shit and the best advice I can give you is to not fucking touch me." I left her standing there, snot mixing with tears. I had to get out of there before I did something to her with my baby there.

I sat in my truck and dialed Bella a few times, but she sent me to voice mail, and I knew she was done playing games with me. I felt that loss in my fucking chest and it hurt. I hit Grip next. "Yo, let's go take care of that problem wit the house now instead of later," I said speaking in code. I wanted to kill Jax, he could get all this rage I was feeling, and I could get my fucking bread back.

"Cool, I will see you there in an hour." I hung up and drove around for a while before pulling up on the block where this nigga was hiding. It came as no surprise that a bitch would be his downfall. He treated these women like they weren't shit and now it was coming back to fuck him up. Karma was a bitch. I met Grip outside the house, and I swear he was happy as fuck to get rid of Jax. I guess I always kind of knew it would come to this, it was just a matter of time. We crept through the backyard and just like Kisha said the back door was unlocked. I walked into this fat mahfucker eating a steak at the kitchen table. He didn't even realize we were there until I had the AK pointed at his head.

"You enjoy that last meal son," I said as he damn near choked, then swallowed. He didn't say shit as I cracked him in the back of the head before kicking him to the floor. He was dazed but, didn't show fear in his eyes. He was probably still thinking about that steak.

"I aint telling you where the money at, so do what you got to."

I laughed, causing the sound to echo in the kitchen. I sounded evil as fuck, and inside I felt the same way. "Bitch, I already know where the money is," I said, and he finally looked scared. I know he didn't think I was keeping him alive to find my money. He should have known better.

"So, you really going to take my life because of a bitch? A treacherous one at that?" I knew Bella wasn't like that, he was just saying whatever the fuck he could to get under my skin. "Yea, I knew you wouldn't believe anything bad about your precious Arabella. But if she so fucking perfect, why did she hide your daughter from you all this time? She played you out like a bitch. Got you around shorty and everything and never once told you that was your kid." I kicked him in the mouth causing a few of his teeth to fly onto the floor.

"You a hater even going into death," I spat. I felt myself

losing control. He should have left Bella out of this. He knew were he fucked up.

"Naw, I aint no hater son. You a stupid mahfucker. You think because the little girl doesn't have your weird ass eyes, she aint yours. But everyone see's it. She is damn near your fucking twin. Walk like you, got that that wide ass nose and pointy ears. She still hot like her mother though. In a few years, she going to be taking dick like a champ." I blew his face off after that, he knew I was going to kill him the minute he said something about Jael.

"Clean up is on the way." Grip said holding his burner phone. "You good?" His eyes were concerned, and I was confused.

"I kill nigga's all the time, hell yea I'm good."

"That wasn't what I meant. But you know what forget it."

"Naw, you got something to say get it up off ya chest." He looked uncomfortable, and I knew right away. The shit Jax was saying was right. Jael did have my mannerisms, I just thought it was because she had spent time with me. I did a mental inventory and realized she did look like me.

"Yea, that nigga was talking some real shit. I mean I thought you knew she was yours, it wasn't my business so I left the shit alone."

My phone vibrated and Bella's name popped up. I hit reject and she called right back, but I just turned the shit off. She knew all these years I had a kid out here, had me around her like I was some random ass nigga. All these bitches were scandalous as fuck.

~BELLA~

Fuck Sire and his bitch. I shouldn't even be as mad as I was. I knew better, I told him I wasn't beat for this side chick shit. But I backslid and now I was sitting here with hurt feelings again. I couldn't blame a fucking soul but myself. I looked at the tickets to Master Chef Live on the dresser and decided I was still going. I wasn't about to fuck up my evening because of him and his bitch. I really needed more friends. Eternity couldn't come because she was keeping Jael and I could have asked Sire's sister but not after what happened today. So, I had to go solo.

I hopped in the shower and turned the water as hot as I could get it. I was so sleepy I almost opted to stay home in the bed. Lately all I wanted to do was eat and sleep, it was probably the way Sire was dicking me down every minute of the day. I grabbed a Red Bull to try and get some energy. I stayed in the shower until the water ran cold just thinking about all the things in my life I wanted to change for the better. I would be graduating soon and then I would be able to begin my career. Shit maybe me and Jael could move away from here and start over. Hopefully Eternity and Cassian would come with us. I could live with out a nigga but my bestie I didn't know.

I felt a pain in my back so strong it caused me to grab on to the towel rack. I hope I didn't fuck up my body having all that rough sex. The pain passed and I stood back up so I could get ready. But by the time I reached for the lotion the whole bottom half of my body felt like it was being ripped apart. I had to sink to the floor or risk falling and splitting my head open on the edge of the sink or tub. I laid there, curled into a ball, crying out in pain. I didn't know if I should call and ambulance or maybe try and use the bathroom. I could feel it was wet in between my legs and I wondered if I had peed on myself. But then I saw the blood dripping onto the floor and I knew what had happened. I was having a miscarriage. I didn't even know I was pregnant, how the fuck did this happen?

I mean I knew Sire basically refused to wrap up when we were fucking, but I was on the pill. This should have never been a possibility. I couldn't take care of another baby, but it didn't mean I wanted my baby to die. I would have figured shit out and loved my child anyway. I was sobbing now for another reason. I didn't even feel the pain anymore. I just felt the loss. My soul was tired, I was tired. I reached for my phone and called Sire, I needed someone to help me. But it just rang out. Then it went straight to voicemail. I forgot his girl had to come before me. I wanted to call an ambulance, but suddenly I felt to weak. What was I even fighting for, my baby was already dead?

TO BE CONTINUED

Made in the USA
Monee, IL
15 July 2021